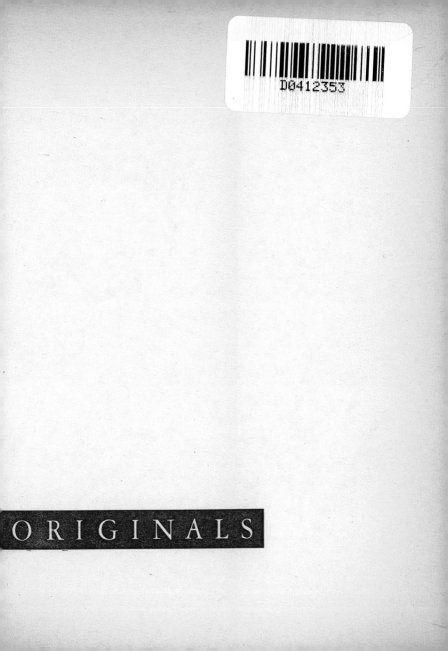

ORIGINALS

IN THE EYES OF Mr FURY

PHILIP RIDLEY

PENGUIN BOOKS

PENGUIN BOOKS

Published by the Penguin Group
27 Wrights Lane, London w8 5tz, England
Viking Penguin Inc., 40 West 23rd Street, New York, New York 10010, USA
Penguin Books Australia Ltd, Ringwood, Victoria, Australia
Penguin Books Canada Ltd, 2801 John Street, Markham, Ontario, Canada l3r 1b4
Penguin Books (NZ) Ltd, 182–190 Wairau Road, Auckland 10, New Zealand

Penguin Books Ltd, Registered Offices: Harmondsworth, Middlesex, England

First published 1989

Made and printed in Great Britain by
Richard Clay Ltd, Bungay, Suffolk
Typeset in 10/12pt Lasercomp Bembo

For my Mum and Dad
— love I've known since life began

PART ONE

A FLY ON THE ICING

Chapter One _____

I WAS SEVENTEEN years old when the Devil died. We found his body on my eighteenth birthday. A fly on the icing was the omen we needed.

For as long as I could remember we had called old Mr Martin 'the Devil'. His real name was Judge Martin, although he had nothing to do with the law. Judge was his christian name. The name that's on his birth certificate. Or so I've been told.

I was told a lot of things about old Judge Martin as I grew up; that he boiled babies and ate them with cabbage, that he kept bats and snakes in his bedroom, that he changed into a werewolf when the moon was full, and that – scariest of all – if I was naughty he would take me from my parents and keep me a prisoner in Hades. My mum told me all these stories. I think it must have been my mum who started calling him 'the Devil', although I can't be sure. Certainly she hated him. And it was certainly my mum who referred to his house as Hades.

'Don't go anywhere near the Devil,' she would tell me. 'He feeds kids like you to his pet monster. And when he's finished with you he makes lampshades and soap out of you . . . He's a demon. Every time you make me cry he puts a cross beside your name in a big black book. When you've got enough crosses he can take you from me. And I won't be able to do a thing about it.'

'Can he _do_ that?' I would ask.

'Of course.'

'And he's really got a monster?'

'Yes. I told you.'

'Have you seen it?'

'Of course.'

'What does it look like?'

'Oh, terrible.'

'But where does he keep it?'

'Every house has room for a monster.'

'But dad would stop him!'

'Listen, my boy. I had a child before I had you. And the Devil took him from me.'

We would squirm and giggle and clutch at each other, shivers running up and down our spines like electric spiders.

Of course, I never believed these stories. And mum would try her best to suppress a smile as she told them. They were just an excuse for her to talk about Judge Martin. He fascinated her. Like he fascinated us all. He was just so ugly. In the summer he would walk around in a filthy string vest and we could see his back and shoulders, covered in hair. He would shuffle up and down the street in his slippers like some monstrous hairy caterpillar. And it wasn't just his back that was hirsute. He had hair everywhere: fingers, ears, even on his nose. It wasn't an enormous leap of the imagination to believe him a were-wolf. He was half beast already.

When I was a child, about five or six, I used to play knock-down-ginger on the Devil's door with Loverboy. Sometimes we dared each other to knock and count to seven before running away. One day, just as I reached four, the door swung open and the Devil caught me. I can still remember my fear as I saw him standing there. There were crumbs in his black beard. Funny how my young eyes took so much in: the sleep in his eyes, his flies open, the way he blinked when he saw me, surprised almost, as if *I* was the ghost, the barely human. Terror must have burnished the image on to my brain with the clarity of an icon. For the first time in my life I knew what it meant to be shit scared. I nearly crapped my pants as I stood there. But I couldn't move. My feet were stuck to the pavement. I heard Loverboy scream at me from the corner:

'Run! Run!'

Suddenly the Devil roared and took a step forward. The smell of his breath was foul. I've no idea what brimstone smells like but I'm sure it was on the Devil's breath that day.

I yelled in fear and flew to Loverboy. I repeat: I flew. To this day I'm sure my feet didn't touch the ground for the whole length of the street. Sometimes the impossible *does* happen.

Loverboy and I took refuge in the Castle. The Castle was our own private hideaway. No one knew about it. Not as far as we could tell anyway. It was in the cellar of an old house that had – to the best of our knowledge – never been lived in. Certainly it was empty when my mum was a girl and she'd lived on the street all her life. Loverboy and I named it the Castle because it looked like a place where vampires might hide. We were obsessed with monsters and ghosts. It was our joint ambition to be horror actors one day. We created a world of our own in that desolate Castle. It was not unknown for us to spend all day in there, enacting scenes from the cauldron of our infant imagination. Loverboy was always the vampire to my priest. It was always my job to exorcize the evil.

I had been friends with Loverboy Tallis for as long as I could remember. His mum was pregnant with him when my mum carried me. The story goes that every time the two women got together Loverboy and I would twist and kick in our respective wombs as if trying to get at each other. 'Even before you were born you were friends,' my mum was fond of saying. And I think she was right. We were – or so I've been told – due to be born on the same day. But my mum was scared by a sonic boom one morning and I was premature. That's how I got my name. Mum says that it was Lover-boy's father, Dicky Tallis, who first thought of it. He had a feeling for names. Look at his son.

But I'll tell you my name later. I mustn't rush things. Everything will be told, but slowly. As it was revealed to me, a bit at a time, almost grudgingly. Names are important. Things begin with names. When I'm ready to begin I'll tell you my name.

I've been thinking a lot about beginnings lately. Beginnings and endings and stories. And how, in a strange way, they simply don't exist. Or rather, if they do exist, then they're variable. There is no truth. Just interpretation. For example, I think of my birth, inspired as it was by a metal bird cooing like thunder, as a kind of beginning. But it's also an end as well. I was already dying before anything had begun. I was already an epilogue as I punched my way through a prologue of blood in order to touch my Loverboy Tallis.

All the time I thought I was living my childhood, my story, I was merely a decorative sub-plot in the lives of others. I thought Faith Niven was my mother but, instead, I was merely her child, her echo. I was something she invented – some kind of metaphysical hom-unculus – and my sole purpose was to give her memories, memories she felt safe with. Perhaps she hoped that, in time, the good memories would destroy the bad. Or at least camouflage them. Oh, I don't know. Perhaps I'm being unfair. I don't know.

This I remember.

One day there was a noise in our street. A scream of car tyres like a feline roar. We rushed out of the Castle to see what had happened. There was a large car half up the kerb. The driver's head was a crushed strawberry through the windscreen. Under the front wheel was a little girl. It was Ruth Enders. Women were screaming. The street belonged to the women and children during the day. The men were all at work. Invisible somehow.

The child lay helpless under the front wheel. She was unconscious.

There wasn't a mark on her face. No blood, nothing. She was breathing deeply and slowly. As if she was sleeping. Suddenly her mother rushed from the end of the street, screaming, scattering her shopping behind her. Now Mrs Enders was about my size at that time and I wasn't big for my age. She was a thin, sickly looking woman. A good sneeze might finish her for good, my dad used to say. And this plucked chicken of a woman rushed up to the car, bent down, and lifted it off her child. Lifted the car high. It might have been made of cardboard for all the effort she put into it. A few women pulled Ruth Enders free. There was blood over her left leg and thigh. But she was alive. The mother put the car down – it was a black Jaguar with glinting chrome – as gently as she could. As if it was made of porcelain.

I *saw* this happen. Now I *remember* it.

Anyone's capable of anything, you see. We're forever on the brink of a miracle.

And so I lived my childhood on the street of women, where men were invisible, where the Devil crawled like a hairy caterpillar with breath like brimstone, where mothers lifted killer Jaguars from helpless children, where metallic birds enticed babies from wombs with coos like thunder, where I hid in the castle of vampires with my Loverboy Tallis and where, on my eighteenth birthday, a fly landed on the pink icing of my birthday cake and told me the Devil was dead.

My name is Concord Webster.

Chapter Two _____

'JESUS! ANOTHER FLY! It's like a plague or something. I've never seen so many,' said mum, plucking one from the sticky icing. She threw it into the love-lies-bleeding. 'Horrible things. They'll be the death of us all.'

We were sitting in the back garden having my birthday party. The air was still and heavy with the smell of flowers. It was one of the hottest days I had ever known. A veritable inferno, my dad called it. The cake dried on our cardboard plates before we had a chance to eat it.

'Happy birthday, darling,' said my mum, kissing me on the cheek. She ran her fingers through my long red hair. 'Beautiful,' she said. 'Beautiful hair.' Then she kissed me again. 'Happy birthday, sweetheart.'

'Yes. Many happy returns,' said Ivy Tallis.

'Congratulations,' said Angel.

I went bright red.

'Don't blush, you silly,' said Ivy.

'He's shy,' said mum.

'Oh, how can he be shy with a mother like you.'

'He's got my good looks. That's the main thing.'

'He takes after his father, Faith Webster, and you know it.'

'Well, he's got my nose, thank God.'

'But they're his father's eyes.'

'Oh, yes. They're Ronnie's eyes alright. Let's hope he sees better times than us.'

'Now you haven't done too bad.'

'Not done too good either, Ivy.'

'What more do you want? A lovely husband, a lovely son, lovely home. You're lucky, Faith Webster, and that's a fact.'

'Oh, you're right. You know I look at some and I feel ashamed of moaning. Count your blessings, that's what my mum used to say.'

'That's right. You've kept your looks for one thing. You're still the most beautiful woman around. Present company excepted,' she added, smiling at Angel.

Angel grinned back.

'Where's your better half today?' asked my mum.

Angel went to answer but Ivy got there first.

'He's helping his dad in the shop,' she said. 'He'll start there full-time at the end of the summer. Might as well get some practice in. And he needs some pocket money. After all, there's that engagement ring to save up for. Eh, Angela?'

'Yes,' she said. 'I suppose so.'

'You're a lucky girl,' said my mum. 'No doubt about it. Lover-boy's a treasure. I bet he lives up to his name as well, eh?' She laughed. 'Listen to me! Talking like this in front of the boy's own mother. I could open a vein. If I were twenty years younger I'd be after him myself.' She touched the beehive of her hair. A style she had had since before my birth. 'Come to think of it, though. I'm not too bad now. You'll have to come round and set it for me again, Angel.'

'You're a siren, Faith Webster, and that's a fact,' said Ivy. She finished her wine and burped. 'Oh, dear. I think I'm getting tipsy.'

'I should think so too,' said mum. 'You've successfully finished that bottle all by yourself.'

'Don't talk daft. I'm not the only one drinking.'

'You are. Connie and Angela haven't touched a drop.'

'You've had your belly full.'

'This is the same glass I started with.'

'It might be the same glass but the contents have changed a few times.'

'It's the same, I tell you.'

'Your nose will grow.'

'I'm completely sober, Ivy Tallis.'

'Then why are your eyes red?'

'Are they?' She pulled a compact from her blouse pocket and clicked it open like an instrument of torture. She studied her eyes. 'Okay. I'm pissed.'

'Such language. In front of your son.'

'He's heard worse.'

'Who from?'

'*Your* son probably.'

'Loverboy doesn't swear.'

'Of course not, Ivy. I was forgetting what a saint Loverboy is. Forgive a poor sinner.' She poured another drink for them both. 'My son is eighteen years old.' Her eyes filled with tears. 'Ivy, does it seem like eighteen years?'

'Oh, don't.'

'Do you remember?'

'Oh, don't.'

'Eighteen years. Why, it only seems like yesterday that we were taking Loverboy and Connie over the park.'

'Don't.'

'Feeding the ducks.'

'They were such beautiful babies.'

'No trouble at all.'

They were both dabbing tears from their eyes.

I looked at Angel.

She smiled.

'Is Loverboy coming here later?' she asked, softly.

'Yes,' I said. 'About seven, I think. We're going to get really pissed.'

'I've got to baby-sit tonight. Mum and dad are out on the town. They can't leave Paul alone.'

'Too bad.'

'Yes. Too bad.' She smiled.

'Listen. Are you okay?'

'Oh, yes.'

'Nothing wrong between you and Loverboy?'

'What makes you say that?'

'Nothing.'

'Has he said anything?'

'No. Just asking.'

'Well, everything's fine. Same as always.'

'That's good.'

'Mmm.'

'Well, isn't it?'

'I suppose so.'

'Now then you two!' said my mum. 'What are you whispering about like snakes in the grass. Plans and plots at the birthday table.' She paused for a while, then added, 'And pots and pans in the kitchen.'

The two women screamed with laughter.

Angela and I laughed as well.

'Oh, look,' said Ivy. 'Just look at the time. Got to go. Your Ronnie'll be home soon. He won't want to see me here when he gets in from a hard day's work.'

'And I've got to get his dinner ready,' said mum. 'Look. Jesus wept. More flies. Something's dead around here. I swear it is. Probably another cat down the chimney like last time. Remember that, Ive?'

'Oh, don't.'

'All that smell?'

'Oh, don't.'

'For weeks on end?'

'Oh, don't.'

'And then Dicky pulled that cat down from up your old chimney. Shoved his hand right up and just pulled it down. Oh, what a sight. I'll never forget it. All those flies and maggots.'

'Oh, don't, Fay. It makes me feel sick just to think of it.'

'Have another drink, then.'

'No. I must go.'

'You're right. Connie. Thank Mother Ivy for your present.'

'Thanks, Ivy,' I said. 'It was lovely.'

'Oh, you're welcome, sweetheart. Thanks again, Faith. Don't forget it's Loverboy's birthday next month. We'll have a little get together at my place then.'

'Without the flies, I hope,' said mum.

'Yes. Let's hope so.'

Mum went into the house with Ivy Tallis. I could hear their voices become fainter as they moved from kitchen to hallway towards the front door.

I turned to Angela.

She was brushing crumbs from the front of her clothes. There was something nervous about the gesture, as if her movements did not belong to her. She smoothed the creases from her lemon-yellow dress.

'What's wrong?' I asked.

'Nothing's wrong, Connie.'

'Well there is. I can tell.'

'Why does everyone think they know me so bloody well? Oh, I'm sorry, Con. Really. I'm sorry. On your birthday as well. Something is wrong. But I don't know what it is. Honestly. I don't. It's just all this, I suppose. Ever since I can remember we've had your birthday party here in your back garden. There's always been the same people. This year is the first one that Loverboy's ever missed. But usually there's you and your mum, Loverboy and his mum and me. Ever since I can remember people have been telling me that I'm going to marry Loverboy. And now I am. I'm just waiting for that bloody engagement ring everyone keeps talking about. Oh, I don't know. It's as if I've had no choice. No say in the matter at all. I'm eighteen. I work in a hairdresser's. I just *do* things. But they have nothing to do with me. Not really. Not where it counts. Do you know what I mean? It's as if we're born and everything is planned for us. This is how it will be. We have no choice in the matter. We all live here on this bloody street. Where our mums and dads lived. And our mums and dads were friends when they were our age. And the friends grow up and marry their friends and live in the same houses in the same street. Oh, it all seems so bloody useless somehow

'You know something. No one has ever asked me if I actually *want* to marry Loverboy. Not once. Not my mum. Not my dad. Not his mum. No one. All they ask me is "Has he got you that engagement ring yet?" And I'm just being sucked along with it all. Like a dead fish in a stream. Pulled along with the flow of things. And you know something else? I've never even asked *myself* if I want to marry Loverboy. Now isn't that something. Not once. I've just accepted it like everyone else. I'm going to marry Loverboy because I've always known Loverboy and he'll give me a ring and we'll live in his mum's house. Oh, it all seems so endless. It's just like an arranged marriage. It's got nothing to do with me. The only meaning I have is that one day I'll be Mrs Loverboy Tallis. It's the story of my life. I've never been my bloody self. First I was a daughter, then a fiancée, next a wife, then a mother. But it's just bloody worthless.

'To be fair, I don't think anyone has asked Loverboy either. No one has asked him if he wants to be my husband. It's just our fate, you see. Like it's your fate to be his best friend. These things are so bloody useless. Worthless. Know something, I can't even tell you if I *love* Loverboy. Now isn't that something. I know all there is to know about him and yet I don't know him at all. I know all I need to know to be his wife, I suppose. I know how he likes his tea and how he likes his meals half burnt and how he can't sleep without a lot of weight on top of him. *You* know him better than I do. It's strange. I get on better with you than I do with him and yet I'm marrying him. And he likes you more than he likes me and yet he's marrying me. We're all doing the wrong things, Connie.

'Know something, I feel like a bloody intruder when you and Loverboy are together. It's as if I don't belong with you at all. I feel like an outcast or something. I'm tolerated because someday I'll be his wife. And that's all I'll be. His wife. It's all so bloody pointless. Pointless, useless and bloody worthless.'

I had never heard Angela talk like this before. Suddenly I realized that there was something inside her, something secret, beyond me, something that possessed her like a demon or ghost, that had nothing to do with the way she lived her life. We accept people by what they say and do, I suppose. But sometimes that's the least of it. Hardly anything at all.

'I always thought . . .' I began.

'What did you always think, Connie?'

'Well . . .' I stammered. 'That you wanted . . . things.'

Somehow I felt lost and stranded. Only our best friends can turn a garden into a wilderness.

'That's just it. I do want things. I just haven't had a chance to work out what those things are yet. I'm just a puppet. Dragged along. A doll in a doll's house. Look at you! What do you want, Concord Webster? Tell me. What do you want? Are you going to spend the rest of your life here? Being Loverboy's friend? Is that all you want?'

Mum rushed over to us. Her cheeks were flushed and her eyes red.

She straightened the rings on her fingers and patted the cone of her hair.

'Goodness!' she said. 'I am a little sloshed, I think. Angel, be a cherub and help me clear these things away. Ron'll have a fit if I haven't got his dinner ready by the time he gets home.'

'But mum wants me back . . .'

'Oh, it won't take a minute. I'm in such a palaver.' She went into the kitchen with a pile of cups and plates.

Angela smiled at me.

'I'll help,' I said.

'No. It's your birthday. Anyway, it's not expected.'

As she stood a ladybird landed on the back of her hand. It was as large as a pebble and unbelievably red. Like a shimmering bubble of blood on her white skin. She looked at it for a while. She shook her hand. The ladybird stayed.

I laughed.

Angela made a clicking sound with her tongue, then flattened the ladybird with her other hand. She wiped away the squashed mush with a serviette.

'Why do that?' I asked.

'It bothered me,' she said.

She went into the house.

As I sat in the garden I tried to think back. My memories became as one with the smell of roses and asters. Thoughts can merge with aromas, I suppose, and become a separate entity. A feeling in themselves somehow. The garden was thick and heavy with perfume. It covered everything like a layer of dust. And through this dust I saw Angela as a child. She had hardly changed at all. Except the younger Angela wouldn't hurt a fly. And this Angela killed ladybirds. Somehow she had changed. And I felt cheated and betrayed.

My mum was always saying 'Oh! I've changed so much! I've changed so much!' But what does that mean? Especially coming from my mum who has done everything in her power to achieve just the opposite. She still wears all her sixties clothes: mini-skirts, knee-high boots; still has the beehive hair-style she had as a teenager. And her hair is still the same colour, a rich auburn, a darker shade of my red. And yet 'Oh! I've changed so much!' So how has she changed? If not outside, then inside. As a cocoon remains unaltered while inside an ugly mush transforms from caterpillar to butterfly.

All my life, if Loverboy had been my best friend, then Angela had been a close second. And I always thought I loved her. She was simply part of my life. There to perform certain functions, do certain things. And one of these things was to marry my Loverboy Tallis.

I stood up and collected some flowers from the herbaceous border, slitting through the stalks with my fingernails. I cut some of the crackerjack marigolds, yellow gladioli, pink asters, a single tiger-lily, then surrounded the central bunch with a haze of baby's breath and highlighted the orange of the marigolds with a sprinkling of blue lobelia.

When Angel returned to the garden I gave her the bouquet.

'For you,' I said.

'Oh, Con. It seems such a waste.'

'It'll brighten up your room.'

'It'll bring on Paul's asthma.'

She shared a room with her five-year-old brother, Paul, who was, as far as I could tell, constantly ill.

'I hoped it might cheer you up.'

'Oh, Con. Yes. It has. Don't listen to anything that I say. I'm okay now. You know how things are.'

'Yes. I know.'

'Well. Got to get back. Mum and dad are going out tonight. I want to make sure I'm there when they go otherwise Paul will panic. They just leave that kid by himself when I'm not there. It's terrible. They know what he's like. Listen. When you see Loverboy tell him to come round and see me when you've finished with him. If it's not too late, that is.'

'We'll be pretty pissed.'

'Don't let your mother hear.' She laughed. Kissed me. 'Happy birthday, Con.'

'Thanks.'

She left me alone.

I folded up the collapsible table and chairs and laid them against the brick wall.

I heard the front door slam shut.

Wait for it, I thought.

'Well,' said my mum, wiping her hands on a tea-towel. 'Nice of you to give half the garden away I must say.'

'A few flowers . . .'

'That we won't be able to see again.'

'She was depressed.'

'*I'm* depressed. I don't see anyone go out of their way to give me a bunch of flowers. I'm nothing but a servant here.'

'Look at the garden, Mum. It doesn't look any different. I bet you can't even tell where I got the flowers from.'

'Of course I can. Do you think I'm blind? I've got eyes.'

'Where then?'

'There!'

'No.'

'Well, there.'

'No.'

'Well, just wait till your father gets home. He'll notice.'

'He's not bothered.'

She picked at some fluff that had got stuck behind a diamond in one of her rings.

'It's just that I'm thinking of you,' she said. 'You spend so much time in the garden . . . getting it to look so beautiful all the time. Not to mention the money. And then just to dig it all up like that. Kill them for no reason.'

'They're not dead.'

'Well, we can't see them so they might as well be dead.'

'Oh, for God's sake.'

'Okay, okay. I won't say another word. I'm afraid to open my mouth most of the time anyway.'

I laughed and picked her a white rose.

'For you,' I said. 'Another death.'

She smiled.

'Oh . . . you little sod!'

She chased me round the garden. We were both giggling like school kids. When she caught me she tickled my ribs.

'You'll hurt yourself,' I said.

'I'll hurt *you*, my boy.'

I screamed with laughter and fell to the floor.

'You're a sod,' she said.

'I'm not!'

'What are you?'

'Stop! You're killing me.'

'Tell me what you are first.'

'But I mustn't swear.'

'I'll allow it this time.'

'No!'

'What are you?'

She tickled me so much I thought I'd have a fit.

Suddenly there was a ringing at the front door.

'Well,' said mum and stood up, brushing the grass from her legs. 'Saved by the bell, young man.' She looked down at me. 'Your hair is so beautiful, Connie. Really it is. Mine used to be exactly the same colour when I was your age.'

She went into the house.

Still gasping for breath I stood up. There was grass everywhere, down my shirt, up my nose, in my ears. I sneezed and coughed.

I became conscious of voices in the house.

Still coughing I went inside.

Mum was standing by the front door talking to old Mama Zep.

Mama Zep was about four feet high, dressed entirely in black, had long hair dyed vermilion and was – at least – eighty years old. She looked nearer a hundred to me, though. Her face was wrinkled and yellow, lipless somehow, like a monstrous lizard. She was the witch of the street. She was also our local fortune-teller, magician, doll-maker, herbalist and anything else you cared to name. Most women refused to see the doctor when they could visit Mama Zep. She had potions for every possible ailment that she kept in empty pickle jars. Her voice never grew beyond a calm, rasping whisper, a kind of hypnotic whispering sound. If vipers could talk, they would sound like this. She had delivered most of the people now living in the street. When pregnant women began their labour they screamed for Mama Zep.

As I walked up to them I heard Mama Zep saying,   '. . . and you know it, Faith Niven.'

'It's nothing to do with me any more,' said my mum.

Mama Zep smiled.

'It's always going to be something to do with you, Faith Niven. You know it and I know it. Now I don't want any more fuss. Why knock down a good door?'

'I'll wait till Ronnie gets home.'

'No. Let's do it now. Before the men arrive. Death and birth are women's work. You know that. You know what women do.'

'Call the police. If you're so sure.'

'But there's no need. Why bother them? It's nothing. What's a death? Hardly anything at all. Natural. Nothing to be afraid of. We can go and take a look. Make sure!'

'You're an interfering old harpy, Zep. You always have been.'

'It's the penalty I pay for knowing too much. Now stop being a stupid girl. Please get it.'

My mum hesitated for a second, looked at me, then rushed upstairs. There was a look in her eyes I had never seen before. Horror, perhaps.

'What's going on?' I asked.

'Well, let's see,' Mama Zep whispered. 'It's like this, Concord Webster. Suddenly you realize that you haven't seen someone for a while. You know what I mean? And that's what I thought this morning. About someone.'

'Who?'

'When was the last time you saw Judge Martin?'

'The Devil?'

'Yes.'

'Oh . . . last week. No . . .'

'You see? When you get to be my age you know all the signs. I've seen it before. Death stays the same. It may be weeks since anyone's seen him. And, of course, no one would miss him. No job, nothing. You see – ah! it's all so simple – he's dead in there, Concord Webster. The Devil is dead in Hades. I can smell it through the letter-box. As dead as stone. I just want to make sure.'

'Yes?'

'And there's no need to knock down a good door. That's what the police – the *men* – would do. No! We women can handle it a better way. We have our secrets.'

'But why come to mum?'

'As I say. Don't want to knock down the door.'

'Yes?'

'So I come to Faith Niven.'

'Yes?'

'Your mother has the key to the house, Concord Webster.'

'Oh, you're wrong. She doesn't even know the Devil. Why would she have the key to his house?'

Mama Zep smiled.

'Don't want to knock down the door to Hades, do we,' she whispered in my ear. 'Who knows what monsters might fly out.'

'But . . .'

I rushed up to mum.

She was in her bedroom, standing by the dressing-table. As I entered she slammed one of the drawers shut. She was shaking all over. Her face frozen and expressionless. She looked like some hideous zombie.

'Mum . . .'

'What?' she snapped. 'Get out! Get out of here!'

'But . . .'

'I said get out!'

I left her room.

After a few seconds she came out and thrust a key into my hand.

'Here,' she said. 'You go down there. I can't. You go down with the old witch. I've done my bit. I'm going to bed. I feel ill.'

She slammed the door behind her.

I stood in silence for a while, then went back to Mama Zep.

'Ah, you've got it. She's a good girl at heart.' She smiled. 'No need for you to come with me. I can do it myself. We don't want any fuss. No one will bat an eyelid to see me go in. Just give me the key.'

'No,' I said. 'I'll come with you.'

'Well, if you want to.' She grinned at me. 'Tell me. Have you ever seen a dead body before?'

'No.'

'Or been in love?'

I frowned.

'No,' I said.

'Then this will be quite a birthday for you, Concord Webster. Give me your handkerchief.'

I gave it to her without question.

We started to walk down the street towards Hades.

'It'll smell to high heaven in there,' she said, pulling a bottle from her cardigan pocket. 'I can smell it from here. Can you? No, I suppose not. I wasn't so eager to smell death when I was your age either. But I'm nearer to it myself now, you see. We're almost neighbours. Believe me, I've had worse.' She sprinkled some rose-water on to my handkerchief and gave it back. 'Breathe through this when we get in there. It will help. We don't want any fuss. No crowds. We'll just go in, open the windows, make sure. Can you smell it yet?'

'No,' I said.

'You will. Are you afraid of rats?'

'Rats!'

She smiled.

'Oh, the innocence of it all. The innocence. Oh, don't worry. Death is nothing. The same as birth. Nothing. You live, you have babies, you die, they die. Nothing to be afraid of. Nothing unnatural. Just the way of things. A dead body. You wash it, dress it, bury it, mourn it. Although I don't know who'll mourn for young Judge Martin. Those who would have mourned are gone now. But I'll put flowers on his grave. You see, I have to do this. I brought him into the world. So I'll see him out. I'll be his mourner. I'll do what his son should do.'

'His son?'

'Why yes.'

'He has a son?'

'Am I the first to tell you about young Judge's son? Fancy.'

It was strange to hear her refer to the Devil as young. For me he had always been old Judge Martin, the Devil. A name that was a person. A person I hated because I was told stories about him. Stories that became a name that became a person.

'Yes, I'll put flowers on his grave,' she continued. 'These rituals have to be observed.'

'But everyone hated him,' I said.

'Really? Did you hate him?'

'I . . . well . . .'

'But you didn't even know him. You didn't know him as well as . . . well, as well as you know your own mother, for example.'

'No,' I said.

Once, when I was about eight or nine, I went into Mama Zep's house. It was like going into a charmed cave. Every room was full of dolls and toys. A lifetime of make-believe. A lifetime of no life somehow.

'We're here,' she said. 'Can you smell it?'

'No.'

'Open the door.'

I hesitated.

'Hurry up,' she said. 'You've got the key.'

Still I hesitated.

'Oh, give it here.' And she snatched it from me.

She opened the door.

Immediately a smell so intense and sickly came over me that it stuck to the back of my throat like an unctuous membrane.

'Told you!' she said, triumphantly.

I covered my mouth with the rose-water handkerchief.

She gave me back the key.

'Keep this,' she said. 'You might need it sometime. Listen. You don't have to come in.'

'I want to,' I said.

'Oh, the innocence of it all,' she said. 'The innocence.'

The hallway was exactly the same as I remembered from my

knock-down-ginger days: yellow walls with peeling paper, the dustbins, piles of shoes, the newspapers, the empty tin cans. The house
was as dark as a cavern. All the lower windows had been covered
with corrugated iron. Fingers of light probed through cracks in the
metal, cutting dusty shafts through the ghostly rooms.

We looked in the living-room: sofa, table, television, everything
covered in a carpet of dust. There were tins of food everywhere.
Boxes of them. As if he had been preparing for some impending
apocalypse. The house was like a wilderness.

There was a noise from a dark corner. A rustling.

'Stamp your feet!' commanded Mama Zep.

And we stamped our feet as if we were cold. Which, by the way, I
was. The house was as cold as the grave.

'There!' she said. 'Listen.'

Throughout the house there was a strange sound, a scampering of
tiny feet. Poltergeists, I thought.

'Rats, my dear,' she said, almost affectionately.

My blood turned to ice.

'Come on,' she said. 'He's upstairs.'

All kinds of nightmares filled my mind. Stories I'd heard about
rats eating babies, about rats running up trouser legs and doing
unimaginable things. I trod carefully.

Mama Zep, on the other hand, was undeterred by either the
rats or the smell. She stomped up the stairs as if she owned the
place.

We stood outside the bedroom door.

I could barely breathe by now. The smell was simply devastating.
My stomach gurgled and my eyes watered.

'Men are no good when it comes to death,' she said. 'Just look at
you. Always the women that have to deal with death. Always the
women that wash the bodies and plug the holes.'

I tried to look a little braver.

She opened the bedroom door. It swung open silently as if by sorcery.

'Mother of God!' hissed Mama Zep.

How can I describe this? Words are impossible, you see. Is it enough to say I threw up the moment I saw . . .? No. That is not enough. Is it enough to say that even Mama Zep staggered back? No. That is not enough. Nothing is enough. And so, in the end, the event is rendered useless, meaningless.

The room was dark, but there was light enough to see. A single shaft of sunlight illuminated the room.

He lay on the bed like an embalmed gargoyle. He was naked and his whole body was black with dried blood. There was a dark halo on the sheet around his neck and head which was obviously caused by the blood that had run from the wound in his throat. His neck had been slit from ear to ear, the wound grinned at us like a second mouth. There was a knife clutched in his left hand, glinting in the golden light, blood on silver. His whole body was encrusted with flies and maggots like a second skin. Three rats were nibbling at various parts of his body and, as we looked, a fourth jumped on to the bed and stared at us like a gloating succubus. His genitals had been eaten and flies fed on the disgusting wound. The insects glittered over his body like black ice or polished ebony, glinting blue and green off their shiny backs. The Devil lay there like a sacrifice.

'Mother of God!' exclaimed Mama Zep.

The flies flew from the body. It was like a snake shedding a dead skin. They swarmed around the room like a plague of locusts. They flew into my face, into my mouth, blinded me, made me sick.

'Mother of God!'

Mama Zep started to open the windows.

I ran out of the house.

There were a few people outside by now. I fell into the gutter and vomited again. Dead flies swam in the bile.

I stood up.

The smell stuck to me. The women around me covered their noses and pulled their children away from me as if I was infected, a leper almost.

'What's happened, son?'

It was my dad.

He sniffed.

'Copped it, has he?'

I nodded.

'I think he . . . I mean it looks like he killed himself,' I stammered.

'Runs in the family from what I hear.'

I vomited again and spat some more birthday cake and flies into the gutter.

'Is Mama Zep still up there?'

I nodded.

'I'll go up, then. Go home and see if your mother's okay. I left her in bed.'

My heart was still pounding. All I wanted to do was have a bath. Wash away the sins of others. I felt obscene.

I went home and knocked on my mum's bedroom door.

'Come in.'

She was in bed, staring blankly at the ceiling.

'He's dead,' I told her.

'Are you *sure*?'

'Can't you smell it?'

'I smell it.'

'He's dead.'

'You never can tell,' she mumbled.

'He's dead!'

Suddenly she sat bolt upright. There was something warped and spiteful in her eyes. She clutched the sheets with hands like talons.

'You can't be sure!' she screamed at me. 'You can't be sure until there's a stake in the vampire's heart. Do you hear me? Until there's a stake in the Devil's heart!'

Chapter Three _____

WHEN I WAS younger I suffered from a sequence of recurring dreams that made my nights a kind of torture. Sleep was just another doom for me. A death almost. These nightmares plagued me for years. A few times a week I would wake up screaming, the sheets twisted and stuck to me. My parents would rush into the room.

'Was it a story?' my dad would ask.

'Yes,' I would answer. 'A story.'

And so, in my mind, stories and nightmares became as one. Each story is a sort of nightmare to someone. I was taught that at a very early age. As I lay there, breathless and shaking with the terror of my dreams, I realized that all stories possess a certain pain. When the Devil gets bored he tells stories to his bats and these bats fly to us and give us these stories as nightmares.

'Was it a story?' asked my dad.

'Yes,' I answered. 'A story.'

'What one was it this time?'

I was sitting in an open, circular arena. It looked like a circus. An empty trapeze dangled above my head. In the centre of the forum was a Punch and Judy show. Punch was hitting Judy with his stick. She was screaming and pleading with me to help her. Blood trickled from her nose and mouth. But I was powerless. Invisible hands held me firmly in my seat.

'I can't move!' I screamed.

'Try!' begged Judy.

Suddenly Judy's screaming stopped and when I looked up Punch was eating her.

I ran from the circus and found myself in a zoo. A long corridor of cages lay in front of me. The cages did not contain animals though. Behind the bars I recognized familiar faces: mum, dad, Loverboy, Ivy Tallis, Angela.

They were all sitting in front of television sets, watching the screens with expressionless faces.

'Did you like the show?' asked mum, without moving her eyes from the flickering light of the television.

'Judy is dead!' I cried.

'You'll meet her again. If you want to meet her again.'

And then, quite suddenly, my mum peeled her face off as if it was a mask. Underneath a monster snarled at me. It was green and scaled like a giant lizard or dragon.

'I love you,' said the dragon.

I screamed and started to run. There was a light at the end of the corridor. Someone was waiting for me in this light. I could see him quite clearly. It was a man with a shaved head. His scalp gleamed in the light.

But the corridor of cages just grew longer in front of me. There was no end. I could hear snapping bars, then footsteps behind me. I was being chased.

I always woke up as the first deadly claw grabbed my shoulder.

'Was it a story?' my dad would ask.

'Yes,' I would answer. 'A story.'

Chapter Four —————

WHEN LOVERBOY CAME round at seven o'clock he had his mother with him.

'How is she?' she asked my dad.

'Upstairs,' he answered. 'Still in bed.'

'Is she asleep?'

'Just staring at the ceiling.'

'Poor lamb. She was alright this afternoon. We all had a wonderful time. Has she said what it is?'

'No.'

'Haven't you any idea?'

'No.'

'Well, have you called the doctor?'

'She doesn't want one.'

'But Ron . . .'

'She doesn't *want* one, Ivy. I've asked her. What more can I do? She's not a child.'

'Well, can I go up?'

'Help yourself. See if you can talk some sense into that skull of hers.'

She smiled at me, squeezed my arm and went up to mum's bedroom.

Dad disappeared in the kitchen.

I looked at Loverboy.

'There's something going on,' I said.

'Oh, yeah? What?'

'I don't know. But . . .'

'You have . . .'

'Suspicions. Yes.'

'Mmm. Sounds interesting. Tell me about them.'

'Not here. Have you got . . .?'

'Two bottles of wine. At the Castle. Waiting for your pleasure.'

'And?'

'Oh, your present. Of course.'

'Of course,' I said.

I had known Loverboy for so long that I no longer saw him. In a way he was invisible to me. Like you get used to a smell. After a while you don't know it's there at all. Loverboy was like that. So when someone says to me 'Oh, yes, Loverboy Tallis. He's the boy with only one eye,' I have to pause and think before replying, 'Yes. That's right. He's only got one eye.'

Perhaps it's guilt on my part as well. But, somehow, I don't think so. I don't notice anything about Loverboy any more. He's simply my best friend. But because looks are important, because looks make the person – or so I've been told – I will try to describe him.

Imagine this:

a boy, nearly eighteen years old, with blond hair scraped back from his forehead and combed into a smooth seal-skin over his skull, brown eyes, olive skin, a wide, infectious smile, red check shirt open at the neck, bleached denim jeans, white running shoes, silver crucifix dangling from left ear, black eye-patch over right eye. These are the things that make the image of Loverboy Tallis.

'Come up to my room for a second,' I said.

'But I just want to get drunk.'

'It won't take a second. I just want to show you the mask.'

On the desk in my room there was a dragon mask I had been

working on. It lay there like some prehistoric legacy, a fossil of papier-mâché and chicken wire. The flour and water glue had dried to a white film over the newspaper, giving it the appearance of bone. I had just started painting the green skin, a scale at a time. The eyes were two holes in the mask. Wherever you stood in the room the eyes watched you.

Loverboy sat on the bed.

'It's looking good,' he said.

'Mm. Not bad,' I said. 'I'm quite pleased with the way it's going.'

'What are you going to do with it when it's finished?'

'Well . . . Nothing. I'm just going to make it.'

'But what is it for?'

'To wear. To look at.'

'But why?'

'I don't know what you mean, Tal.'

'Well, it must be for something. Yes? Everything has a meaning. Yes?'

'Yes. I suppose so.'

'Well then? Oh, I don't know. I know you're cleverer than me and all that. Perhaps this is all above my head. You've just been spending so much time making this mask. And I was wondering if there's any point to it, that's all.'

'Yes. There is, Tal.'

'Tell me what it is.'

'You wouldn't understand.'

'Just because I've only got one eye doesn't mean I see half as well as you.'

'I know that.'

'Oh, forget it. It doesn't matter. If you say it means something then that's good enough for me. I just want to get pissed tonight. I've had a hard day at the shop. Shall we go?'

'Yes.'

Suddenly we became aware of muffled sobs coming from mum's bedroom. Ivy Tallis was trying her best to comfort her.

'See what I mean,' I said. 'Something's going on.'

'What?'

'Judge Martin killed himself.'

'Well, I know that much.'

'He's been dead for ages.'

'I know that as well.'

'I went down and found the body with Mama Zep.'

'What? Mama Zep was in bed with the corpse of old Judge Martin?'

'Don't joke about it, Tal. You know full well what I mean.'

'Yeah. Okay. I know. You'll have to tell me all the gruesome details. What did it look like?'

'Like hell,' I said.

'I hear there were rats.'

'That's right. They'd eaten . . . No! Listen. There's more to it than all that.'

I stopped for a while. The crying had ceased next door. I could hear Ivy Tallis's voice, level and reassuring. Like a parent soothing a child.

'How do you mean?' asked Tal.

I walked over to the window and looked down into the garden. Again I smelt the flowers.

'Is Angel okay?' I asked.

'What's she got to do with it?'

'Nothing. Listen. My mum had the key to the house, Tal. Can you believe that? My mum had the key to old Judge Martin's place. And all evening she's been crying. Or just staring at the ceiling. Mumbling. It's the first time she's not cooked dinner for my dad. He's really pissed off about it all. But why, Tal? Why should my mum have the key?'

He gave the impression of thinking for a while. The eye-patch moved against his cheek as he frowned.

'Perhaps . . .' he began.

'Yes?'

'Well, I don't know. What do you think?'

'I don't know either. But when Mama Zep was talking to my mum I heard her say something about it always having something to do with her. My mum that is.' I sat on the bed next to Loverboy. 'Tell me. How old do you think Judge Martin was?'

'Oh, I don't know. I've never thought of it. Devils don't have an age, do they?'

'Make a guess.'

'I can't. Sixty?'

'No. I think he was younger. You know what I think?'

'Tell me.'

'I think he was about our parents' age.'

'Well, he looked a lot older.'

'That's right. You know what else I think?'

'What?'

'I think that, years ago, my mum and the Devil were . . .'

'Come off it, Connie.' And he giggled, slapping my leg with the flat of his hand. 'You can't be serious.'

'But I am. It's what I think.'

'Oh, but it can't be true.' He peered at me with his one good eye. 'There's one person who'll tell you all the secrets,' he said, softly.

'Yes,' I said. 'Mama Zep.'

'Mama Zep,' he echoed.

We sat looking at each other. The room was still and ominous. The eyes of the dragon watched us from my desk.

There was a tapping at my door.

'Yes,' I said.

Ivy Tallis came in. She walked over to the bed and sat down.

Her eyes were red and swollen. There was a shredded tissue in her left hand.

'Connie,' she whispered. 'Your mum's very ill. I don't know what it is. She won't tell me. Is everything alright here?'

'As far as I know.'

'No arguments?'

'No more than usual.'

'Then I don't know what it is. She's just lying there.' She dabbed away some more tears. 'I'm afraid to leave her alone, Connie. I really am. What could have happened? She was alright this afternoon. What's happened since then to cause this?'

'Judge Martin,' I said.

'Oh, he's nothing to do with it. Why should she bother about that old devil? I know her better than that.'

I wanted to cry with her. But I couldn't. All I could do was sit and look at her. Waiting.

Ivy stood up.

'I'll go and see if your dad's okay,' she said. 'Has he had his dinner?'

'Yes. I cooked him something.'

'You're a godsend, Connie.'

She tiptoed out of the room.

'Well,' murmured Loverboy. 'This looks serious.'

'I told you.'

'But your mum *hated* Judge Martin.'

'So she said.'

'All those names she called him.'

'Sticks and stones,' I said.

'You think she was lying?'

'No. I don't think that. I just don't think she told everything. I think she did hate him. But I also think that, at one time, she did not hate him.'

'You mean loved him.'

'I don't know really. But I think so.'

I put my shoes on and we left the bedroom. Before going downstairs I looked to see if my mum was okay.

The room was still in darkness. She was curled up in a fetal position beneath the sheets.

'Mum?'

'Mmm?'

'Do you want anything?'

'No.'

'Shall I stay in?'

'No. Go out.'

'I won't be late.'

'Mmm.'

I closed the door.

Downstairs dad was doing the washing-up. He smiled when he saw us but there was something beneath the surface that scared me.

'She'll be alright,' he said.

'Oh, yes,' I said.

'It's her time of life. Women get like this. You'll see. In the morning she'll be right as rain. Back to her old self. All this fuss. Anyone would think it was the day of judgement or something.'

I was glad to get out of the house. It was like leaving something deformed behind me, something injured. A grief almost. I felt burdened by something that was not even part of me. Something that felt like a guilt. I closed the front door and shut the grief in. Or locked myself out. Either way, I felt better.

Loverboy and I made our usual way to the Castle; round the back of the street, across the dump, then through a strange tunnel of corrugated iron we had constructed to mislead the curious. There was a secret entrance at the back of the Castle that was – as far as we knew – known only to us.

We had made the basement of the Castle our own private domain. Over the years it had been filled with the flotsam and jetsam of our lives: old toys, comics, wine bottles, an old sofa we found on the dump, a television set with its insides blown out and, in their place, a plastic human skull. Some masks I had made decorated the walls. There was an old wooden table in the middle of the room. The table only had three legs. Where the fourth leg should have been we had nailed a broken guitar to keep it upright. On the table there was a headless doll sitting on a top hat. There was a plastic carnation sprouting from the doll's neck. When you pulled a string in the doll's back the flower said, 'Sorry mummy . . . sorry mummy . . .'

I felt more at home here than anywhere else. The Castle was mine. Part of my mind somehow. Getting drunk with Loverboy in this part of my mind was my greatest joy.

Loverboy poured two glasses of wine.

'Cheers,' he said. 'Happy birthday, old man.'

'Thankyou, baby.'

We downed our drinks in one.

'And now . . .' He went to the bright pink cupboard in the corner of the room. 'To prove that the cupboard is not bare.' He gave me a square parcel wrapped in glinting gold paper. 'Your birthday present!'

We sat on the sofa.

Loverboy poured some more drinks.

I tore the paper away. Inside there was a black box. I shook it. Something rattled inside. It felt solid and heavy.

'What is it?' I asked.

'Open it and see.'

I removed the lid. Tissue paper. I scattered the paper around us like confetti. Inside there was a glass dolphin. It was blue and sparkling.

'Oh, Tal.'

'You like it?'

'Of course I do.'

'Thought you would.'

'You just know me so well.'

'That's my misfortune, I suppose.'

'Come on. Let's get legless.'

By the time we had finished the first bottle it was getting dark outside. Loverboy lit the seven candles on the candelabrum we had soldered to the top of an old gas cooker.

'How are you and Angel getting on?' I asked.

'That's the second time you've mentioned her tonight. What is this? Do you fancy her or something?'

'Don't joke, Tal.'

'Okay, okay.' He flopped down beside me. 'Right then. How is Angel? Let me think. Angel is fine. Why? Don't you think she's fine?'

'I'm not sure.'

'You worry too much, Con. That's always been your trouble. You go looking for heartache and melodrama the whole time.'

'I've always thought it looked for me.'

'Nonsense. You never believe it when anyone tells you they're happy. You were like that when you were a kid.'

'I wasn't.'

'Oh, you were. Don't forget. I was there.'

'Well, I was there too. You don't know me as well as you think, Tal.'

'Yes? Well, I know more about you than anyone else.'

'That's true.'

'So?'

'So what? Just because you know more about me than anyone else doesn't mean you know me. A little bit more than nothing is still next to nothing, you know.'

He looked at me. His one good eye filled with tears.

'Oh, shit.' I said. 'I'm sorry, Tal.' I put my arm around his shoulder.

'Why are you in such a fucking bad mood all of a sudden?'

'I'm sorry.' I pulled him closer to me. The smell of his aftershave intoxicated me more than the wine. He had been wearing this brand ever since he started shaving. Every time I smelt it I thought of him.

He laid his head on my lap and I ran my fingers through his almost white hair. It was sparkling with grease. I smoothed it flat, comforting him. I felt his breath against my legs.

'I'm sorry,' I said again.

We must have slept for a while because the next thing I knew the candles were nearly out.

'Tal? Tal?'

'Mmm.'

'Come on. I think it's late. I promised Angel we'd go and see her. She's baby-sitting.'

Loverboy sat up and shivered.

'It's cold,' he said.

We tapped lightly on Angel's front door.

'You two look bloody awful,' said Angel when she saw us.

'We've been drinking,' said Loverboy.

'I can see that much. Come in. I'll make you some coffee.'

From upstairs we could hear Paul's asthmatic breathing. It sounded painful.

'He's been like that all night,' said Angela, filling the kettle with water. 'I just don't know how he sleeps. I've done all I can for him. I've given him a few puffs from his inhaler and opened the window. There's a bowl of bleach beside his bed. That helps, so I've been told.'

'But how?' asked Loverboy.

'I don't know. Mum says it does.'

'But in what way?'

'The fumes, I suppose.'

'How?'

'Oh, I don't know, Tal. Ask mum. If she ever gets back.'

'When did they say they'd be back?' I asked.

'An hour ago. I spend half my life baby-sitting for them. It drives me mad some nights, you know. Paul's breathing. I end up wheezing in bloody sympathy sometimes.'

'He can't help it,' said Tal.

'Oh, I know he can't help it, Loverboy. But that doesn't stop it driving me up the bloody wall, does it.'

'Keep your hair on.'

'Then stop trying to piss me off.'

'You're pissing yourself off.'

'Oh, for fuck's sake!' And she rushed out of the kitchen. We heard her footsteps run up the stairs and into the bedroom.

'What's wrong with everyone tonight?' asked Tal.

'Are you sure it's not you?'

'I haven't done anything.'

'Exactly.'

'What's that supposed to mean?'

'Oh, nothing, Tal. Forget it.'

'Everyone's going mad.'

'Go up and see if she's okay.'

'No. Let's go. I don't like all these scenes. Let's just go. I'm tired now. She'll be back to her old self in the morning.'

'And she'll have a bastard of a night. Go up and tell her you love her.'

'She knows that.'

'Does she?'

'We're going to get married, aren't we.'

'Tal . . .'

'Okay, okay. But wait here. Yes? Don't go. I won't be long.'

'I'll wait.'

He went upstairs. I sat in the cold light of the kitchen and listened to the hypnotic rumblings of their muffled voices.

After a while Angel came down.

'Lover's staying for a while, Con. He said that you should go. He'll see you after work tomorrow.'

'Okay.' I smiled. 'Is everything . . .?'

'Oh, look,' she said. And dragged me into the living-room. She flicked on the light. The flowers I had given her were in a vase on the television. 'They really brighten up the room.'

'But they were for your room.'

'I can't have them in there because of Paul.'

'Oh, yes. Of course. Well, tell Loverboy I'll see him tomorrow then. Tell him I'll try to meet him after work.'

'Yes,' she said.

'It's been a hell of a birthday,' I said.

She kissed me.

'I love you,' she said.

'Oh, I'm blushing now.'

She opened the door.

'Oh, I nearly forgot,' she said. 'The strangest thing happened earlier this evening. I was looking out of the window and old Mama Zep walks past. She told me about Judge Martin and all that.'

'I'll tell you all the gruesome details sometime,' I said.

'Don't think I want to know. Anyway, she tells me all about it, then she says, "You can tell Concord Webster that he can visit me tomorrow if he wants. I've got things to tell if he wants to hear."'

'Mmm,' I said.

'What has she got to tell you, Con?'

'Stories,' I said.

PART TWO

LETTER TO A
STRICKEN DARLING

Chapter Five _____

'I WILL TELL you things,' whispered Mama Zep. 'If you really want to know. I thought perhaps that it shouldn't be me. That it wasn't my place. But, then again, perhaps it is my place. You see, perhaps I'm the only one who knows everything. I'm the only one who really got to know *her*.'

'Her?'

'The third one. The third of the three girls. There were three of them. Oh, so beautiful. I can still see them now. Your mother, Rachel Sims, and Petra Gerda.'

'Rachel was . . .'

'Judge Martin's wife, yes.'

'Who killed herself?'

'No. She died in childbirth.'

'Oh, yes. The Devil has a child. You mentioned that before. Where is the son now?'

'After Rachel died Judge sent his son to live with Helen Martin, Judge's elder sister.'

'I've never seen the son.'

'He's never been back. Not as far as I know.'

'Where is he? Where does he live?'

'Oh, another place. But Helen will be back. She has no choice. She has to bury her brother. She can't hide him under a pile of leaves.'

'So there were three girls. My mother, Rachel and . . .'

'The third.'

'Yes. The third.'

'Petra Gerda,' she said, smiling. 'Some tea?'

'Oh, yes. Okay. I still don't see where all this is going, Mama Zep.'

'Mmm.'

'Tell me. Did my mother have an affair with Judge Martin when she was younger? Before she married my dad?'

She sat opposite me and chuckled.

'Oh, my sweet little Connie. It's not as straightforward as that. It would be nice if it was, wouldn't it? But love is never simple. Love involves people and people are complicated things.

'Listen. I'm an old woman. I've seen all there is to see on this street and it still means nothing to me. The older I grow the less sure I become. I've seen ghosts on the street, Concord Webster. Thousands and thousands of ghosts. Each jostling the other for space, for time. And each ghost is grieving and sad. Sometimes I watch them at night from my bedroom window. The street looks like a market, it's so full of the dead. They walk aimlessly up and down. Daughters calling for mothers, mothers for daughters, lovers for lovers. All the sad lost. I want to help them but there are just too many. That is what the past is like, Connie.

'You see, we are all born with a certain magic. I believe this to be true. Not magic like walking on water and things. But a magic that enables us to be wonderful. To be special. Now if you suppress that magic, stifle its growth it turns sour and gangrenous inside you, grows like a snake, until you become a kind of monster. A devil, if you like.'

'Is that what happened to Judge Martin?'

'In a way.'

'He lost his magic?'

'Or had it taken from him.'

'By who?'

'By . . .'

The kettle whistled on the gas stove. She tapped my hand, smiled and went to make some tea.

Her room was full of dolls and toys. Shelves full of marionettes watched me from the walls. The house smelt of dust and honeysuckle. In the centre of the room was a table covered in a lace cloth. On the cloth there was a crystal ball.

Mama Zep gave me a cup of tea. It was as red as blood.

She nodded and smiled to herself.

'My full name is Zeppelina Rosaline Black. I tell you this because names are important. I was named after the Zeppelins my mum adored so much. It was quite a common name then. Or so I've been told. Zeppelin for the boys and Zeppelina for the girls. I've never met anyone else with the name, though. So, perhaps, I'm the only one left. Perhaps I was the only one to begin with. Who knows? All names are unique.

'My mother used to call me her Black Rose. And that's how I started to see myself. As a black rose. The way you see yourself is important, you see. It's as if you carve yourself out of your own interpretation. And so I became the name I was called. I was the Black Rose of the street.

'I saw my first ghost when I was about six or seven. It didn't scare me. I didn't know what it was, you see. It was a bright summer's day and I was playing in the garden and this old man came up to me. He was a very nice old man.

'"Hello," he said to me.

'"Hello," I answered.

'"You don't know me, do you?"

'"How did you get into our garden?" was all I could say.

'He told me that getting into gardens was the least of his worries. Oh, we spoke for ages. He played with my toys and said that he used to like dolls when he was a child.

'"But boys don't like dolls," I said.

'He smiled and said something. I can't remember what it was. After a while he said he had to go. I asked him to come back and he said he certainly would. Before he left he gave me a message to give to my mother.

'When I went back into the house mum said that she had been watching me from the scullery window.

'"How did that old man get into our garden?" I asked.

'"What old man?"

'"The old man I was playing with."

'"But you were alone, darling."

'"No. He's been out there for hours."

'My mum smiled.

'"He gave me a message for you," I said.

'"What was it, dear?"

'"He said that you were still his Little Angel of the . . . the . . ."

'"Flowers?" finished my mum.

'"Yes. That's it. Flowers."

'She held me in her arms.

'"Oh, God!" she cried. And the tears trickled down her cheeks. "I can smell him. Oh, daddy, daddy, daddy."

'And I tried my best to comfort my mother as she lay helpless on the scullery floor.

'You see, I had seen her dead father, my grandfather, who had died before I was born.

'That was how I discovered my magic.

'But all magic is different, you see. No two people have the same kind of magic, just like no two people feel the same kind of love. There are all kinds of magic and yet we only have one word for it. All language is worthless and yet we stammer on.

'Now, you're wondering what all this has to do with the story of Judge Martin and the three girls. Well, in a way, it has nothing to do with it. But, on the other hand . . .' She smiled. 'I knew them all, you see. Faith, Rachel, Petra, my little Judge. I knew them all. I was present at three of their births . . . I saw them all scream their separate ways into the world. Including Petra. Petra was special. Apart from the rest. And yet, in a way, she was the most perfect. The most wonderful.' She sipped her tea.

Outside I could hear children playing in the street. I watched them through the lace curtains.

Mama Zep nodded.

'Yes,' she said. 'The laughter of children. It never changes. It's the same for ever. The same as crying. Though no two people ever cry in the same way. That's why it's always so hard to understand people. We assume that everyone feels the same things that we do. But they don't. Not always. Perhaps not ever.'

'You still haven't told me . . .'

'I know. But I've begun to tell you. That's the important thing. Look out of the window. Look. What do you see?'

'Children playing.'

'And?'

'Cars, dustbins, a black cat.'

'But you've missed the most important thing. The one thing that's always been there. When you look out of the window the main thing you see is the street. It's the same street it's always been. More tea?'

'No. I'm fine.'

'Where shall I begin. Have you ever heard the name Jessica Silver?'

'No.'

'She married Gabriel Martin.'

'So she was Judge Martin's mother?'

'Yes. Let's go back that far. Years ago there was a beautiful girl and her name was Jessica Silver. She was such a shy, sweet little thing. Everyone was in love with Jessica Silver. I knew her when she was a girl. She was such a charming little thing. She had a laugh like tinkling bells. I can still hear her laugh sometimes. A beautiful sound.

'It had always been taken for granted that Jessica Silver would marry Gabriel Martin. And that's what happened. They moved into their new home and, just before the war, Jessica gave birth to her first child. A girl.'

'Helen,' I said.

'Yes. Helen. Helen was very much like her mother. Shy. A bit of a loner. Serious. And she had that tinkling laugh. Though there was always a darker side to her. A certain melancholy.'

'And when the war was over?'

'Gabriel Martin came back from the war and he was a hero. He had lost an eye, you see. Oh, but something had changed inside him. I could feel it at once. There was something inside him. He had secrets. He had done things. I could feel it, Concord Webster, I could feel it. There was evil there. Heaven knows, he wasn't an angel when he went away. We all knew that. But he was certainly a monster when he got back. I suppose he had seen things. Horrors. And these things had become part of him. People were scared by Gabriel Martin even while they liked him. He was capable of anything, I always thought. I could see it in his eyes.'

She poured herself another cup of tea. She dunked her biscuit in the blood-red liquid and sucked at it with her reptilian lips.

I waited.

She smiled at me.

'The day Gabriel Martin got back from the war he told Jessica, his wife, that she was going to have a child. She would have no say in the matter, no argument. She was going to have another child whether she liked it or not. That was that. If necessary, he would tie her to the bed. And this time it had better be a boy or else. Jessica told me all this. She was so scared. She wanted help. But I couldn't do anything. I was as helpless as she.

' "You're going to give me a son," he said.

'And that's what she did. A son. A beautiful child.'

'Judge Martin,' I said.

'Yes. Judge Martin.' And she smiled. 'The baby Judge Martin.'

Mama Zep ran her hand over her bright red hair. She sighed. She looked at me and smiled.

'Judge Martin,' she said. 'What was it you used to call him?'

I hesitated before saying, 'Oh, lots of things. The Devil . . .'

'The Devil. Yes. The Devil.'

'Was Judge his real name? The name that's on his birth certificate? Do you know?'

'Do I know? Yes. Yes, I know. You see, I named him.'

'You?'

'Yes. I gave the Devil his name.'

'But how?'

'Listen. I'll tell you about the night he was born. I can still remember it all so clearly. There was a birth and a death that night. In a way. As there would be a generation later. Everything repeats endlessly. Things always come back to haunt you. We don't get away with anything, Concord Webster.

'You see, it was quite clear to me that Gabriel Martin was as mad as a jumping goblin. He took to drink, gambling and beating his wife. But that's no sign of madness in a man. Quite the opposite. Most men take to drinking and gambling and beating their wives around here. But . . . oh, the stories poor Jessica would tell me. I think she feared for Helen, you see. The first child. Helen must have been seven or eight by the time Judge was on the way. And I think she was afraid that Gabriel might interfere with her. Sexually that is. Oh, he was a brutal man. Wicked. Something inside him made him a true monster. Not a monster like . . . like Judge eventually became. But a true monster. A monster that sucks all the joy out of your life.

'Jessica asked me to keep Helen here as much as possible. And that's exactly what I did. Oh, she was a lovely child. I had grown to love her as if she was my own. Really. She was a special child. And she hated her father. I've never seen such hatred in one so young.

'One day I saw him drag her the whole length of the street by her long black hair. She screamed and kicked him the whole time. From inside their house I could hear her screams as he took the belt to her. And then the yells of Jessica as she pleaded with him to stop. And then the screams of Jessica as he took the belt to her as well. The next day there would be cuts and bruises all over them. While he went to the pub with his mates to get pissed and laugh about it all. And forget about his troubles, he said. His troubles! Ha! There was nothing inside Gabriel Martin except his secret. The secret that ate his life away.

'And so that was the situation we find ourselves in when Jessica Silver was ripe and bursting with her new son. And it would be a son, you see. Gabriel's evil annunciation would prove a prophecy. "You will have a son," he said. And that's exactly what she did.

'But . . . oh, I want to describe this so carefully. The night that Judge Martin screamed his way into the world is so important. So prophetic. Oh, yes, everything was an omen that night. I should have seen the signs. I should have protected him. But I was helpless. Fate, Concord Webster, fate.'

Around us the ticking of the clocks seemed to grow louder until the sound filled the room. Became deafening almost. The ticking clocks became one with the smell of honeysuckle and the stories that flew like bats from the lipless mouth of Mama Zep.

'When someone is in trouble,' she said, so low I could barely hear it, 'you take them and put them in a magic circle. Yes, you draw a circle around them. This circle is the compass of love. If you do this, they are safe. But if they are not protected they succumb to the night.

'Gabriel Martin kicked Jessica down the stairs one night. Why I don't know. No one ever knew. Not even Jessica. He didn't need reasons, you see. He just did things. After he had kicked her down the stairs he locked her in the coal cupboard. Her screams woke me. I went to the house. I nearly knocked the door down. I could hear Jessica screaming, "Broken . . . broken . . . broken . . ."

'Gabriel opened the door.

'"Let me in!" I demanded.

'"This is none of your business, you old gorgon," he said. "Go back to your cave."

'"This is where I belong, Gabriel Martin," I said. "Unless you want your son born in a hole like a rat."

'Reluctantly, he let me into the house. I opened the cupboard door. Jessica was screaming. Some neighbours helped me carry her to the bedroom.

'As she screamed a storm swirled in the sky. Yes, there was thunder as Judge Martin pushed his way into the world. The worst storm I'd ever known. Rain lashed against the windows. There was lightning. I was scared that night, Connie Webster.

'The labour was long and bloody. When the boy was born there was a caul over his face. An opaque mask. I removed it. He had thick black hair and eyebrows. I'd never seen such thick hair on a babe before. I bit through the umbilical cord and held him, slippery with blood, in my arms. I held him and whispered, "You're here now. It's all begun." And he opened his eyes and started to breathe. He didn't cry, you see. No need for tears. He just opened his eyes and started breathing. And he looked at me. I swear this is true. I remember it, Connie Webster. He looked at me and smiled. And his eyes said, "Yes. I am here. Will it be wonderful?"

'"Oh, yes," I answered. "Wonderful, my angel, wonderful."'

Mama Zep started to cry. She wiped the tears away from her eyes with a black handkerchief. She looked at me and smiled.

'Oh, so silly,' she said. 'To cry after all these years. But the tears are still part of it all. What does it matter? Nothing.

'And when I laid the child in Jessica's arms I noticed a strange thing. Jessica's hair was white. As white as snow. As if the birth had drained her of colour. Turned her into a ghost, a phantom. But she was happy. Happy with her child.

'"Look at his eyes!" said one of the neighbours. "And his hair. A little devil . . ."

'"No!" I said sharply. "Not a devil. Don't ever call him that. An angel. Say it. Don't ever let him believe himself to be a monster."

'"What shall I call him?" asked Jessica. "I haven't even thought of it."

'"We'll have to be careful," I said. "Names are powerful. They possess magic. They judge us by our names."

'Jessica smiled and said:

'"Then that's what I'll call him. Judge."

'And that's how Judge Martin came to be.'

She stood up and went over to a shelf of dolls. She smiled and touched a few of them affectionately. Their white, expressionless faces stared back at her.

'You know,' she said, 'it could be that these are not merely dolls. Not only toys. They could be effigies. Sometimes I feel like that. That each of these dolls I make contains the soul of someone on the street. And that it's my duty to protect them. I'm their guardian, if you like. I'm in control of their future.'

She came back and sat down in front of me. There was a strange atmosphere in the room now. Spiritual somehow. As if I was taking part in some ritualistic ceremony.

'Jessica was never well again. But that didn't stop Gabriel from being the monster he was. Somehow he realized he had an easier way to hurt his wife now. A baby. I remember this all so well. One day, in the midst of an argument, he grabbed the baby from its cot and dangled it from the open bedroom window. Dangled it by its feet like a turkey. He threatened to let the child fall to the pavement below. He threatened to kill his own child. Oh, he was mad now. Sometimes I held the baby and there were burn marks over its beautiful legs where Gabriel Martin had stubbed out cigarettes. Oh, how I feared for those children. For Jessica as well. No one was safe with him in the house. No one.'

She looked out of the window and smiled.

'But there were the birds, Concord Webster. That was the first sign I had of the magic inside my little Judge. The birds. Jessica would put him outside the front door in his pram and the pigeons and sparrows would fly down to him. Of course, the mother was scared. All the mothers were. They thought the child was in danger. "His eyes," they said. "His eyes. The birds will peck out his eyes." But it soon became obvious that this was not the case. The birds simply wanted to be near Judge Martin. He called them to him. In his silent way, he spoke to them. And they sat on the hood of his pram and nestled in his blankets. And they followed him as Jessica wheeled the pram to market. And I knew . . .'

She touched my hand. Her skin was cold as ice. She smiled.

'I believe Judge Martin killed Gabriel. Oh, not directly. But he killed him none the less. He killed him as surely as if he had put the gun in his father's mouth and pulled the trigger. Listen. Judge learned to speak at a very early age. He picked everything up so quickly. I'd never seen such an intelligent child. One day he was talking to his father and the child told him . . . something.'

She paused.

'Told him what?' I asked.

'Remember I said that Gabriel Martin had a secret. Something that was, I believe, eating his life away. Eating his sanity away at any rate. Things he had done. Or not done. Something he had seen, perhaps. Whatever the case might be, this thing he told no one, this thing he kept locked in his skull, this thing . . . This thing was known by his son. And Judge Martin spoke of these horrors in his innocent two-year-old voice.'

'But how?' I asked. 'How could he know?'

Mama Zep smiled.

'He just knew them. Who knows how? You see, I think that Gabriel saw Judge – in the beginning at any rate, when he first got back from the war – as a way of forgetting these things. But, instead, he became a way of remembering.'

'But what were they?'

'The secrets?'

'Yes.'

'I didn't know then. And I don't know now.'

'Then what happened after Judge told his father the secrets.'

'Nothing. For a while. Gabriel Martin got drunker and drunker. He screamed at his children. But he no longer hit them. And then, one night as he lay in bed next to Jessica, he turned the bedside lamp on, tapped Jessica on the shoulder, said, "It will all be wonderful," put a pistol in his mouth and blew his head off.'

The room seemed to spin around me.

Mama Zep shook her head.

'Can you imagine? The blood sprayed over the lampshade. The whole room became stained with red light.'

'And Jessica?'

'Oh, she didn't scream or panic. She got out of bed and put her dressing-gown on. There was a crowd forming in the street now. I was part of that crowd. She opened the front door. The children were both screaming.

'"Mama Zep," she says. "Come here please."

'I went with her into the house. She closed the door.

'"Will you take Helen to your place for a while."

'Her face and hair were covered in blood. Like the rest of the street I had heard the gunshot. I thought, perhaps, she was hurt. I grabbed her arms and pulled her to me. There was such clarity in her eyes. I'd never seen it before. Not since she'd married Gabriel at any rate. She had the eyes of a girl again.

'"No," she said, sensing my fear. "It's not me. I'm not hurt. Nor are the children. Gabriel has killed himself. He's upstairs. Please take Helen for me. I don't want her to see."

'"But what about Judge?"

'"He's in the bedroom. He's too young to understand."

'"But . . ."

'"Please take her."

'So I took Helen back to my house.

'When they found Jessica later she was holding Judge in her arms. They were both sitting on the bed and looking at the dead body.

'Now listen . . . The blood stained Jessica's hair red. I mean that. From that day on, until the day she died, she had bright red hair. Just as Judge's birth had drained her of colour so Gabriel's suicide gave it back to her.

'And so she was left alone to bring up her two children. Helen was a wonder, though. She looked after Judge. Nursed him when he was ill. And he was often sick.

'Judge visited me a lot when he was young. Children have always taken to me more than adults. It's the same now as it's always been. And so the young Judge Martin – how old was he? Six? Seven? Something like that – came to see me. He would sit where you're sitting now. And that's how I found out about the dust, the milk and the cups.'

'I'm sorry?'

'The dust, the milk and the cups.'

'I don't understand.'

'I'll tell you about them one at a time. First the dust. For ages

Jessica had been telling me how Judge was afraid of dust. Oh, not dust when it settles on objects. But dust when it's caught in beams of light. You know, when it swirls like fog in a chink of light through the curtains. He would shiver with fear when he saw this.'

'So?' I asked.

'One day he was sitting where you are now and he stared in fear at that corner. The corner where the dolls are.'

I looked at the corner.

'"Dust!" he says to me.

'Well, I looked but I couldn't see any dust. In fact, the room was quite dark at the time.

'"No," I said. "There's no dust."

'But he insisted, "Dust, dust, dust!"

'And then I knew. He wasn't seeing dust at all but something that – to his young eyes – looked like dust. He was seeing ghosts. He had the magic that I had had as a child. He could see the dead. Ghosts were his dust.'

She smiled and nodded at the corner.

I felt a shiver run up my spine.

'I told Judge not to be afraid. That they would not hurt him. The dust was good, harmless. And I think he believed me. His fear diminished. He said the dust spoke to him but he couldn't understand the words. I told him not to worry. One day he would.

'Next, the milk. One day Judge said to me, "I can turn milk sour."

'"Really," says I. "How?"

'"Watch this," he says.

'And he pours two cups of milk from the same bottle. Then he just puts his finger in one of the cups. And – yes – the milk had turned sour. As he handed it to me to inspect it was already green and curdling in the bone-china cup. We tried this a few times. And it worked every time. He could turn milk sour by simply touching it. Mmm. What next?'

'The cups,' I reminded her.

'Oh, yes.' And she chuckled to herself. 'The cups. Of course. One day we had an argument. You know what children are like. Little things can upset them. And Judge Martin was still a child for all his magic. I forget what it was all about. Perhaps I refused to buy him something. I don't know. Anyway, he gets up from his chair and he looks at me and he screams, "I'm never coming back!"'

'And, on the word "back", every cup on the table – and there were quite a few of them – broke into a million pieces and lay shattered on the table-cloth. So you see. Dust, milk, cups.'

'Yes,' I said. 'I see.'

Mama Zep stood up.

'Follow me,' she said.

She led me upstairs and into her bedroom. It was like something from another world. And still there were dolls to watch me.

She brought a black box from underneath her bed.

'Look,' she said. 'Just look at this.'

She removed the lid from the wooden box. Inside there was cotton wool. She rummaged around for a while and then revealed something lying in the soft interior. It was a strange, yellow-ochre thing, like an empty oyster shell.

'What is it?' I asked, reaching out.

'No. Don't touch it.'

'But what is it?'

'This is the caul that covered Judge Martin's face. This is his mask. I've kept it all this time.'

I stared in wonder at the remnant of flesh. An unusual, fish-like smell came from the box and, as I looked, sparks seemed to fly from the dead skin. It was like looking at something sacred. I felt a sense of wonder and awe. The caul was slightly translucent and a prism of colour reflected from its surface.

'It's beautiful,' I said.

'Yes. He was beautiful.'

'The Devil's mask,' I said.

'Look in that mirror there,' she instructed me.

There was a full-length mirror in her wardrobe door.

'I'll have to go,' I said. 'Really. I have to meet Lover —'

'Look in the mirror first. There's time for that.'

I looked.

'What do you see?'

'Myself,' I said.

'Describe yourself.'

'Sorry?'

'Tell me what you look like, Concord Webster.'

'Can't it wait until next time like the rest of the story?'

'Oh, yes. A lot of things can always wait until next time. But not this. This has to be done now. Look at yourself and tell me what you see.'

'I've got long red hair, thick and straight. Beautiful hair, my mum says.'

'Yes,' she agreed.

'My face is pale and ghostly white.'

'Delicate.'

'Sickly,' I corrected.

'Carry on.'

'Grey eyes. Big eyes, wide. Innocent eyes, I suppose. Yes?'

'Yes. I would say so.'

'Slim. Hairless chest. Thin nose. Long arms. Very wide mouth. A friendly smile?'

'Yes. Very.'

'A white shirt, open at the neck, torn denim jeans, black boots, earring in my right ear . . .'

'What is it of?'

'Voodoo skull with top hat.'

'Mmm. Carry on.'

'There's nothing else to say.'

'So that's what you look like?'

'Yes.'

'That's all you can tell me about the way you look?'

'Yes.'

'And if I were to tell you that you looked different from that what would you say?'

'I'd say you were wrong.'

'Good.' And she smiled. 'Don't ever forget that. You've got a beautiful, innocent face, Connie Webster. Don't let anyone ever tell you otherwise. People want to change people. It gives them a sense of power. But don't be changed. You know what you are.'

'Yes,' I said.

As we walked downstairs I said:

'At the beginning of this afternoon you said that this was the story of three girls. But I haven't met one of them yet. My mother is one of them. But . . .'

'Go and meet Loverboy.'

'But . . .'

'You'll have to hurry.'

'Tell me next time,' I said.

'Oh, my dear Connie. There's always a next time.' She opened the front door for me. 'By the way,' she said, 'did you take your reflection out of the mirror before you left?'

I laughed.

'It's not a joke,' she scorned. 'A cat might have nine lives, but we have only one. Our reflection is part of our shadow. If we lose that we become . . .'

'Vampires,' I said.

'Why, Connie,' she said. 'You're becoming quite a sorcerer's apprentice.'

She closed the door.

Chapter Six _____

LOVERBOY WAS JUST closing the shutters in the shop when I got there.

'Come in,' he said. 'God. It's been a busy day. Sorry about last night. Yes?'

'Last night?'

'Just disappearing with Angel like that. Not coming down to say goodbye and all that. Not like me.'

'Oh, that's nothing.'

'You didn't mind?'

'Not at all. She needed you more than I did.'

'Well, I wouldn't say that. But she was in a bit of a state.'

'How long did you stay?'

'Until her parents got back. Sheila was so pissed. God. I'm glad my mum doesn't come home like that. It's not what mothers are supposed to do, is it? I don't think they even knew I was there. I left while they were in the kitchen.'

'Where's your dad?' I asked.

'He's gone home early. It's the rock 'n' roll night tonight. The night when all our dads dress up and try to make out they're sixteen again. It gives me the creeps. Anyway, I'm a big boy now. I can close the shop by myself.'

I sat on the counter and started to juggle with some tin cans.

'How's your mum?' asked Loverboy, ringing the till open.

'She was still in bed this morning. But she looks a little better. Dad stayed at home with her today. I've never known him take a day off work. He's gone in when he's been half dead with flu. So he must be worried by it all.'

'Have you found out what it is yet?'

'No.'

'Did you go to see Mama Zep?'

'Yes.'

'And what did she tell you?'

'Oh, nothing.'

'Nothing?'

'That's right. Nothing. Not yet anyway. Are you seeing Angela again tonight?'

'Yes. We're going to see a film. Want to come?'

'No. She'll get fed up with having me around.'

'Don't be silly. She likes you. You know that.'

'I know, Tal. But she'll still get fed up.'

'Well, I don't see how.'

'Because she wants to go out with you, Tal. Not me.'

'But she is with me.'

'Yes. And you're with me. Look, Tal. She doesn't want me around the whole time. She wants to have you to herself now and again.'

'I don't see . . .'

'I know you don't, Tal. You'll just have to take my word for it. That's all.'

'You're so serious all the time, Con.'

'So everyone keeps telling me. Pretty soon I'll end up believing it myself.'

'So what will you do tonight?'

'I've got some work to do.'

'On the dragon head?'

'Yes. That's right.'

'I still think you should come out with us. We can have something to eat . . .'

'It's like talking to a brick wall talking to you.'

He laughed and put the cash from the till in a plastic bag. I went into the back room with him while he put the money in a safe. Afterwards he sat down and poured some lemonade.

I sat opposite him.

'Oh, yeah. News of the day,' he said. 'Someone's in Judge Martin's house. That's all anyone's talked about in the shop all day. Old Martin dead. Killed himself. Why did he do it? Why after all these years? God! It's been a hell of a day. Yes?'

'Yes,' I said. Then, 'Who?'

'Who what?'

'Who's in the house?'

'A woman.'

'His sister?'

'How did you know?'

'God! Helen Martin is back.'

'Jesus. You know her name as well. I thought I was going to impress you with all this and you know . . .'

'What have people been saying?'

'Oh, that she hasn't been back since she left years ago. By all accounts she went to live in the country somewhere.'

'Where she was evacuated during the war?'

'That's right. Perhaps you should tell me.'

'No. Carry on.'

'By all accounts . . .' A deep breath and a mouthful of lemonade. '. . . her mother . . .'

'Jessica.'

'I don't know her name. Her mother had to send her back to the people she was evacuated with during the war because she was a widow and couldn't afford to keep two children. So Helen went to the country and Judge stayed with his mother here.'

'Did anyone say how Jessica Martin was widowed?'

'No.'

'I see . . .'

'Do you know?'

'No. Not at all,' I said.

'Right. That's that then. Anyway . . . Helen Martin is back in the house. She's been cleaning it out all day from what I hear. There's been lorryloads of rubbish coming out of the house. She's really giving hell a spring-cleaning, eh?'

'By the sounds of it,' I said. 'But are you sure she's alone? There's not someone else with her?'

'Not as far as I know.'

'Then I wonder when he will get here.'

'Who?'

'The son. Judge Martin's son,' I said. 'He's got to have a second coming, you see.'

Mum was still in bed when I got home. I took her a cup of tea. There was an uneaten tray of food on the floor beside her. The curtains were still drawn and the room smelt awful.

It was such a shock to see my mum like this. Her usually immaculate hair was a tangled mess over the pillow. Her hair was lifeless. Without her make-up and hair-spray she was a different person. It scared me somehow. Made me feel vulnerable.

'You have to eat,' I said, sitting on the bed.

'Why?'

'Oh, what is all this?'

'I just don't feel well.'

'But . . .'

'No questions, Con. I feel better today than I did yesterday. And tomorrow I'll feel a little better than I do today. And so it'll go on. Until I'm well enough to get up and resume my normal position. As a servant to you and your father. Where were you this afternoon? With Loverboy?'

'No.'

'Where then?'

'I was talking to Mama Zep.'

She looked at me with fear in her eyes. She clutched at my hand and started to cry.

'What is it, Mum? Tell me. What is it?'

'With that *cow*.'

'Mum?'

She buried her face in the pillow.

'Mum?'

Muffled crying.

'Mum?'

She sat up.

'Listen to me, Connie. Listen to your mother. If she has to tell you, then let her. I can't stop her. I won't stop her. But all she can tell you are stories, you see, just stories. She can't tell you anything about feelings.'

'Is there a difference?' I asked.

'I don't know any more,' she said. 'I don't know. It used to be my protection to think so.'

'I think she's heading for a nervous breakdown,' said my dad as I walked into the kitchen. He was at the sink doing the washing-up. 'Ivy Tallis thinks so too. She's just cracking up, Con. And there's nothing I can do because I don't know why.'

'Dad,' I said, sitting down, 'have you ever heard of the name Petra Gerda?'

'Petra Gerda? No. Why?'

'I just wondered.'

'Who is he?'

'It's not a he. It doesn't matter. She used to live on the street or something.'

'Must be before my time, then. I only moved here when I married your mother, you know that. Ask her about it. She knows everything.'

'Yes,' I said. 'I suppose so.'

'Why do you ask? Is it important?'

'No. I don't think so.'

'Well, I'm going to get the doctor to see your mother whether she likes it or not. I'm not having all this. I've got enough to do without having to deal with all this as well. Missing time off work. I won't even be able to go to old Dicky Tallis's do tonight because of her.'

'Yes you will. I'm staying in tonight. I'll keep an eye on her.'

He smiled.

'You're a good boy, Con,' he said.

'Keep saying it. I might believe it yet.'

That night I worked on my dragon head.

As I sat in my room the smell of night-scented stock drifted into me through the open window. Along with the sounds of rock 'n' roll coming from the Tallis house.

The eyeless dragon stared at me.

'Do you want to see?' I asked. And I looked in my drawer for something to make his eyes with.

The doctor had come in earlier that evening and given my mum some sleeping tablets. She had been in a comatose state ever since. The doctor said she would sleep her troubles away and wake up a new person. I wasn't so convinced. Sleep never erased any of my worries. On the contrary. It merely gave me new ones that my waking state could never fathom.

As I sat there, the smell of flowers merged with the thoughts of

Mama Zep's story. The various images she gave me hovered inside my head, flew out, alive, like sparks, and fluttered around the dragon's head also, joining us in electric communion. In my skull I could see Jessica Silver's white hair, Gabriel's suicide, hair turning the colour of blood, the sour milk, the smashed cups, the ghostly dust, a baby dangling helpless from an open window. All these images revolved inside my head, unresolved, waiting for an end. These stories became real for me. Real in the voice of Zeppelina Black. Who was part of the story as well. Because she was – in a way – the whole of the story. Its centre. The eye of the storm, if you like.

I still couldn't find anything to use as eyes.

'Still sightless,' I said.

I stood up.

Wiping the palms of my hands, I looked in my mum's room to make sure she was comfortable.

The room was dark and smelt of sleep. I never knew sleep had a smell until that night. But it has. A heavy, sweet smell, not unlike death, cloying, hypnotic almost.

I half-closed the door and walked over to the bed. Mum was sucking her thumb. There was a half smile on her lips. She looked peaceful. What was she dreaming? What dreams thundered in her skull as her sleep sent out its sweet aroma?

Beside the bed was her dressing-table. I touched the drawer in which she had hidden the key. I still had the key. It was heavy and solid in my pocket. What else was in that drawer? Where one secret was hidden could there yet be others?

I looked at my mum.

Sleep. Deep sleep. Endless.

Quietly, I opened the drawer: lace handkerchiefs, pressed flowers, empty perfume bottles, and a letter. An old letter.

I closed the drawer.

I tiptoed back to my room.

The letter was simply addressed to 'My Stricken Darling'. I looked inside.

A photograph. Black and white. Square. About twenty years old judging by the clothes. A photograph of three girls. Three girls standing outside the house. Despite the passing of time two things in the photo had not changed. One was my mother. She looked the same then as she did now. And the other was the house. The three girls were standing in front of Judge Martin's house. I looked closer at the image. And a face stared at me through one of the windows of the house. A teenaged boy's face. A face misted by the glass as if it were a ghost. A face. A face.

I felt my heart flutter.

God! I thought. I know who that is. I know that face. Although I had never seen it before. I knew who it was.

Judge Martin.

It was the young Judge Martin.

The young Judge Martin before he was the Devil.

And the three girls stood outside his house, holding hands, smiling, and one of these girls was my mother and one must be Rachel, who was to marry Judge Martin and die in childbirth and the other must be Petra Gerda.

This is the story of three girls, Mama Zep had said. And here they were. The three girls. But she hasn't told me the story yet. She's only told me about the birth and childhood of Judge Martin.

I looked at the back of the photograph. There were four signatures; Rachel Sims, Faith Niven, Petra Gerda, Judge Martin. And then, in block letters, TOGETHER FOR EVER.

Together for ever?

So how long does for ever last? Together might have lasted for ever in the photograph but it certainly didn't last in real life. Out of the four, one was to kill himself, one died in childbirth, one had to sleep her hate away, and the other . . . Yes. The other.

Petra Gerda. What happened to Petra Gerda? What part did she play in all this? This is the story of three girls. One dies, one sleeps, and the other simply disappears.

I put the photograph back into the envelope and removed the letter. Handwritten. Black ink on pink paper. The paper still smelt of perfume. Some things stay, I suppose.

> My Stricken Darling,
> I don't know what else I can say? It's all been said. We have one chance. I'll come for you. You have the power to leave. I give you that power. There is nothing to keep you here. Come away with me and be happy. If you stay here you will go mad. I know it. I know it because I love you . . .

I lay down on the bed.

What did all this mean? I felt I was trapped in a story of someone else's making. This has nothing to do with me. This is not mine. And yet . . .

'My Stricken Darling'. A letter to my mother? Twenty years ago my mother was a Stricken Darling.

Believe, said the dragon. Believe.

This is the story of three girls.

My mother had been in love with Petra Gerda. Is that it? Is that the answer to all the questions? Will knowing this put me in the eye of the storm with Mama Zep? The Black Rose.

As I lay there I dreamed I rode on the back of a flying dragon. As we flew the wind blew scales off the dragon's back. The green scales – as large as oyster shells – turned to sparks in the air and followed us like tiny comets.

'Each spark is a story,' said the dragon.

'Where are we going?' I asked.

'To the eye of the storm. The centre of the hurricane. I'm taking you to meet the story-teller.'

'No!' I screamed. 'I don't want to.'

'Why?' asked the dragon.

'I'm afraid,' I cried.

'Don't be,' comforted the dragon. 'No need. Once you are in the circle that is the centre of the storm nothing can harm you.'

I crawled up the neck of the dragon and looked into its eyes. But black, sightless eye sockets stared back at me as large as caves.

'But you have no eyes!' I screamed. 'How can you find the eye of the storm if you have no eyes?'

'Foolish boy,' said the dragon, its voice a rasping whisper. 'That is my greatest power.'

So we flew on through the cyclone, towards the centre of the vortex, and gradually the winds diminished, faded away, until we were standing in a large, white room. In the centre of the room was a black chair. Someone sat on the chair with his back towards us.

'Go and speak to the story-teller,' said the dragon. 'Tell him all your secrets.'

I climbed off the dragon's back and walked over to the chair.

The young Judge Martin sat there. His beautiful, white face, his coal-black eyes, the thin black eyebrows, the black hair, slick to his skull, sparkling.

'Now listen carefully,' said the young Judge Martin.

'Yes,' I said.

'Once there was a caul.' And he removed his face. Beneath there was the old Judge Martin. 'This caul was a face.' Again he threw away his face. Beneath there was the fish-smelling remnant that Mama Zep had shown me. 'This face was a mask,' he said.

I stood in silence.

'Yes?' he asked.

'Yes,' I said.

'Remove my mask,' he instructed.

'No.'

'Why?'

'I'm afraid.'

'No need to be afraid. Remove the mask.'

I snatched away the caul. It caught fire in my hand and tiny sparks of white light flew away.

Beneath this final caul was my face.

'The story-teller,' said my face.

       'Connie! Connie!' There was a knocking at the front door. I could hear Angel calling my name. 'Connie! Open the door.' Knock, knock, knock. 'Connie!'

'I'm coming,' I called.

I rushed downstairs and opened the door.

'What's happened?'

'There's been a fight. Loverboy sent me.'

'Loverboy's been in a fight?'

'No. Not Loverboy. His dad. His dad and your dad. They've had this big punch-up. Don't ask me what it's about.'

'I'm coming,' I said.

We rushed along the street together.

'Your dad's got a bust nose, I think.'

'Anything serious, though?'

'Oh, no. Don't think so. Dicky has got a few loose teeth and a black eye.'

'But my dad's never been in a fight.'

'I know. Nor has Dicky.'

'And they're the best of friends.'

'Well, I know that too.'

'What could have got into them?'

As we turned the corner I saw my dad sitting in the gutter. He was holding a handkerchief to his bloody nose. There was a small crowd gathered round him. About ten feet away stood another crowd with Dicky Tallis at the centre. In between the two groups was Ivy Tallis.

'Can you believe this?' she cried when she saw me. 'Grown men! Grown bloody men. The fact that they have to wear all their bloody rock 'n' roll drapes as if they're still teenagers is bad enough. But all this fuss. I've never seen the like. You ought to be ashamed of yourself, Richard Tallis.' A few women gathered round her. She looked at her husband. 'It's a disgrace. I could die. I swear I could.'

'Don't upset yourself,' said one of the neighbours.

'Well, I could. My own husband. Acting like a kid. Oh, I could open a vein. I've aged twenty years tonight. Do you hear me, Richard Tallis?'

'Shut up, woman!' he called.

The women sighed.

'You see!' cried Ivy Tallis.

'Are you okay?' I asked my dad.

'Yes,' he said, gruffly. 'Leave me alone.' And then, 'I can't go home like this. Your mother . . .'

'She's out to the world.'

He nodded.

'What happened?' I asked.

'It was him!' said my dad. 'His fault!'

'Liar!' screamed Dicky Tallis.

'You're the fucking liar!' screamed my dad, and jumped to his feet.

There was a commotion as we tried to keep the two men apart.

'Go home, Dad,' I said.

'But . . .'

'Mum's asleep. Just go home. It's best.'

He nodded and walked away.

Gradually the crowd dispersed.

As I stood with Angel, Loverboy walked over.

'What on earth happened?' I asked.

'Haven't the foggiest. One moment it was the same as always. Dancing to rock 'n' roll and all that. Then the next minute all hell was let loose.'

'Grown men!' said Angel.

'Boys at heart,' said Loverboy.

'Monsters more like.'

'Devils,' I said.

'The possessed,' said Loverboy. And giggled.

We said goodnight and made our separate ways home.

Dad was washing his face in the kitchen.

'That man is a bastard!' he said.

'Dad . . .'

'He is!'

'Well, if you're okay . . .'

'Yes. I'm fine. I can handle the likes of Dicky Tallis. If they hadn't have pulled me off him I would have killed him. And they had to, you know. Pull me off. They had to physically pull me off the fucking bastard. They had to beg me to leave him alone. It took five of them to hold me down. You should have been there, son. You would have been proud of your old man.'

'Yes,' I said. 'Well, goodnight, then.'

'That's the end between our two families, you know that,' he said, drying his face on a towel. He seemed refreshed now. Younger, some-how.

'Sorry?'

'The end,' he said. 'I don't want your mother talking to Ivy. And I don't want you talking to Loverboy.'

'But Dad . . .'

'I mean it, Con.'

'But I don't understand.'

'I was insulted in that house, Connie. This family was insulted in that house. Do you understand that? Insulted. That's the end.'

'But Ivy and Tal haven't done anything.'

'They're his wife and son,' he said.

'But they haven't done anything to you, Dad.'

'They're as bad as him.'

'Why?'

'Because they're part of him. They love him. They'll take his side against me. And you. You'll see.'

'But Dad . . .'

'I've got nothing more to say.'

'Dad . . .'

'Go to bed!'

'I'm not going to stop talking to Loverboy.'

'You'll do as I say, young man.'

'You're being silly.'

'What did you say?'

'Silly,' I repeated.

'Go upstairs, son. Go upstairs before I do to you what I did to Dicky Tallis.'

I stared at my father. A different man stood in front of me. Someone I did not understand.

I went upstairs.

'I mean it,' he called after me. 'It's over!'

'Nothing's ever over,' I mumbled as I went into my bedroom. I touched the dragon's head. 'Is it?' I asked.

Chapter Seven _____

I CAN STILL remember another of my recurring dreams.

I was trapped in a black room and, for some reason, I knew that it had to be painted white. I knew that I would not be safe until all the walls were a smooth, flawless white.

Outside the room I could hear voices. The voices were trying to tell me stories but I could not hear them because the walls were black.

'Help me!' I screamed. 'Help me!'

Suddenly a chink of light appeared in the corner of the room. I fell into this light.

I fell out of the black room and into a white room.

There was a television set in the corner. I sat in front of the set and turned it on.

A face appeared on the screen.

'What do you want?' it asked.

'A story,' I replied.

'What do I look like?'

'Black hair, black eyes, white face. Beautiful, wonderful, magical.'

'And do you know me?' he asked.

'No,' I said. 'Not yet.'

'Exactly. Not yet. But you will.'

'Yes. I will.'

'And now for your story . . .'

And I would wake up screaming.

Chapter Eight _____

I WAS STANDING in the shop with Loverboy discussing our parents when a stranger walked in. A woman. She had long black hair with a streak of grey coming from each temple. She was dressed in a bright red kimono and sandals.

'Hello, boys,' she said in an easy, strident voice.

She had the confidence of a battleship.

We nodded.

'Goodness. What a lovely shop. I've never seen so many tins. I haven't been here for years. Not since I was an ankle-biter.' She laughed. 'I've got a few things I need. Who serves me? Or am I going to be lucky and get you both.'

'Me,' said Loverboy.

'What happened to your eye?' she asked.

We both stared at her. No one had ever made such a direct reference to Loverboy's partial blindness before.

'I lost it,' he said.

'Careless you. How did you manage that?'

'I stabbed it out,' I said.

'Really?'

'With a fork,' I said.

'It was an accident,' offered Tal.

'Well, I'm sure it was. Do you deliver?'

'Sorry?'

'Do you deliver? I need this shopping but I can't take it with me now. Can it be brought round to me later?'

'Oh, no,' said Tal. 'We don't . . .'

'Don't worry. I'll come back. What's your name, darling?'

'Loverboy.'

'You're a dish, Loverboy. And that's a fact. Your black patch suits you. You should thank your friend.' She looked at me. 'Who is?'

'Concord Webster,' I said.

'Webster,' she said, softly. 'Yes. Concord. My name is . . .'

'Helen Martin,' I said. 'You're the sister of Judge Martin.'

'That's right. What a clever little Concord Webster you are.'

I smiled.

'When's the funeral?' I asked.

'Tomorrow. You're all welcome.'

'Listen,' I said. 'I have to pass your place later. I could bring your shopping round. If you like. If you want me to, that is.'

'Yes. I would like that. What do your friends call you. Not Concord all the time surely.'

'No,' I replied. 'Connie.'

'Connie. And Loverboy becomes?'

'Tal,' he said. 'From my second name. Tallis.'

'Connie and Tal,' she said. 'Beautiful.' And handed her shopping list to Loverboy. 'Is it okay to pay on delivery?'

'Well . . .' began Tal.

'Yes,' I said.

'Tell me, Connie,' she said. 'Was it you who found my brother? With Mama Zep.'

'Yes.'

'I thought so. It must have been a shock for you.'

'Not really,' I said.

'Mama Zep told me you were sick.'

'The smell.'

'Oh, yes. The smell. It's still there. I've scrubbed the whole place from top to bottom and now I'm painting it. Death stays, though.' She looked at me and smiled. 'Are you Faith Niven's son?'

'Yes,' I said. 'Do you know my mother?'

'No. Not directly.'

As she turned to leave I called after her:

'Is . . . Is Judge Martin's son coming to the funeral?'

'He might,' she said. 'He might not.'

'Is he in the house yet?'

'No. Not yet.'

'But he might come?'

'He might, yes. But he might not.'

'What's his name?'

'Oh, Connie,' she said. 'That would be telling.'

       'Guess who I met today,' I said to my mum. She was out of bed now and watching television in the living-room.

'Who?' she asked.

'Helen Martin. Judge Martin's sister.'

I watched her face eagerly.

There was something inside me, something new, that made me want to torment my mother. She knew secrets, something had happened in her past that she wasn't telling me. It was almost as if I resented her being alive before I was born. As if she had cheated me, deluded me, did not love me enough. And so I threw out comments like these, like tiny fish-hooks to stick in her skin. I wanted to make her suffer. How dare she not be what I thought her.

'Did you hear me?' I asked again.

'I heard,' she said, lighting a cigarette.

'Helen Martin.'

'I said I heard you.'

'Do you know her?'

'No.'

'Not even when you were younger?'

'No. Not even then.'

'But the . . .'

'Oh, go and ask your precious Mama Zep if you don't believe me. I don't know Helen Martin. She's older than me. She was older than Judge.'

'Judge?'

'Judge. Yes. The Devil.'

'I'm going round to see her later.'

'Who?'

'Helen Martin.'

She flicked ash from her cigarette on to the carpet.

'Why?' she asked.

'I'm taking her shopping round to her.'

'Her little skivvy, are you?'

'No. I want to do it. She looks interesting. Different. Anyway, there's some things I want to ask her. There's still a lot I have to find out.'

'I'm sure there is.'

'Sorry?'

'Mmm.' And picked up a magazine.

'By the way,' I continued. 'Do you know the name of Rachel's son?'

Mum stared at the page. But I could tell she wasn't reading. Her cigarette hung loosely from her lips. There was a pained look in her eyes and her hands were shaking. I had hit a nerve. I moved in for the kill.

'You know,' I said. 'Rachel. Rachel Sims. The girl who married Judge Martin. She died in childbirth. She had a son.'

'Yes,' said mum, softly. 'I know.'

'Do you know the son's name?'

'Yes. I know his name.'

I noticed tears rolling down her cheeks.

'Rachel's son,' I said.

'Oh, Rachel . . . Rachel . . .' And suddenly my mum was sobbing into her cupped hands. She said the girl's name over and over again.

I left the room.

The letter and photograph I had stolen from my mum's room were still on my bed. I closed the door and looked at the letter again. Could this letter be from Rachel? Was that it? Were Rachel and my mother lovers? Is that why my mother hated Judge Martin so much? Because he took her love from her?

This is the story of three girls.

Yes. Three.

So where does Petra Gerda come into it?

I could hear the telephone ringing downstairs. Obviously mum was still too upset to answer it. I went down myself.

'Hello,' I said.

'Hello, Con.' It was Ivy. 'Is your mum there?'

I looked in the living-room and mouthed who it was. Mum shook her head.

'She's asleep,' I said.

'Oh, this is so silly,' she said. 'This thing between Ronnie and Dicky, I mean. Do you know that Dicky's forbidden me – I repeat, *forbidden me* – to talk to your mum again. I can't believe all this is happening. Grown men! Us women have got to get together and talk some sense into their thick skulls. We've got to have an atone– at– atone– Oh, what's the word I'm looking for?'

'Atonement,' I said.

'Yes. Exactly. They're grown men. But, there you are, men just never grow up. Is Loverboy there?'

'No.'

'He must still be at the shop then.'

'Yes,' I said. 'Must be.'

'Well, love to mum.'

'Yes,' I said.

And put the phone down.

I knocked on the door. It was green like all the others. Except that some of the paint had peeled away like dry skin to reveal a salmon pink underneath.

Helen opened the door and smiled.

'Concord Webster. You're an angel.'

'Your shopping.'

'Bless you. Come in, come in.'

She closed the door behind me.

'How does it smell?' she asked.

'Okay,' I said.

'Well, better, eh? Come on in and I'll make us some tea.'

We went into the kitchen and she put the kettle on.

Helen Martin had done a wonderful job cleaning the house in such a short time. It was practically stripped bare. All the old, rotten furniture had been taken out. There were buckets of soapy water everywhere.

'What an attractive boy Loverboy Tallis is,' she said.

'Oh, yes,' I said. 'He's my best friend.'

'He's very nice. So you stabbed his eye out, eh?'

'It was an accident. It happened years ago. We were children.'

'How did it happen?'

'We were at a birthday party. His I think. We were just sitting at the table shouting at each other. And I lashed out at him. Only I had a fork in my hand. The next thing I knew his eye was on the end of the fork.'

'His eye offended you and you plucked it out, eh?'

'Accidentally,' I said.

'But of course. One dreads to think what might happen if children went around doing things like that on purpose. And getting away with it. Just think of it. That must be the worst thing, don't you think?'

'What?'

'To do something and get away with it. Just think of it for a while. All that guilt. Building up.'

'Yes,' I said.

'Sit down. Take the stuff off that chair.'

We sat down at the table.

'Not much has changed since I left,' she said. 'Not much at all. Even the people look the same. The same types at any rate.'

'Have you *never* returned since you left?'

'No. Not once.'

'But why?'

'Never felt the need.'

'Not even to see your brother? Not even when . . .'

'No. I never really knew him. I felt no connection. And he became so reclusive as he got older. And I travelled a lot. I had my work.'

'Did you go to his wedding?'

'No. I was in America then, I think.'

'What do you do to travel so much?'

'I'm a sculptor,' she said.

'An artist.'

'Well, I wouldn't go that far. How do you like your tea?'

'Milky and sweet.'

'Oh, you darling.'

She poured me a cup.

'So you didn't know Rachel?' I asked.

'No. I've heard of her, though. Naturally.'

'What have you heard?'

'Stories.'

'What stories?'

'I haven't come back here to repeat old wives' tales, Connie. It was all a long time ago. It doesn't matter that much any more.'

I stared at her. The light from the window blinded me. I blinked. Stars flew in front of my eyes.

'You see,' I said. 'It's been strange. Ever since Judge Martin died things have been different. I think that something happened in the past that made a . . . difference. Something that changed people. Do you know what I mean?'

'Yes,' she said. 'I know.'

'And, in a way, I'm the last of all those echoes. And I have to find out things. And talking is the only way to do it.'

She paused for a while, sipped her tea, played with the beads around her neck.

'It's not for me to tell you anything,' she said. 'Really. It's not my story. Oh, it might have become mine later. But it's not anything to do with me as far as it concerns you.'

'Then it does concern me?'

'If you make it, yes.'

'Mama Zep is telling me.'

'There's not much she doesn't know. And what she doesn't know she'll make up.'

'Eh?'

'Oh, don't worry,' she said. 'That doesn't make it any the less true.'

After a pause, I stood up.

'I've got to go,' I said.

'I see. Come again. Soon.'

'Oh, of course.'

She showed me to the door.

'What an awful colour,' she said. 'When Crom gets here I'll get him to change it.'

'When who gets here?'

'He'll be at the funeral. I found out a little while ago.'

'The son?'

'Yes.'

'His name?'

'Cromwell,' she said. 'Cromwell Martin.'

The next morning I was awoken by the slamming of car doors. I looked out of my window.

The funeral procession was just about to leave. There were only two cars. The hearse with the coffin and one to follow. Someone was already sitting in that car. It was a teenaged boy. And, as I watched, he looked up at me. Through the glass window. And he looked exactly like the young Judge Martin in the photograph I had stolen.

Helen Martin came out of the house and sat in the car beside him.

There was a pigeon in the road beside the car. Just as the car was about to drive away the boy wound down the window and put his hand out. The bird flew up to his hand and was taken into the car.

The window closed.

The cars drove away.

I had seen Cromwell Martin.

I sat down on my bed and looked at the photograph. The two images looked exactly the same. The boy in the house, the boy in the car. I was in love with one of them. That much I knew for certain. I only hoped it was with the one that could be saved.

PART THREE

BANISH BLOOD ON SILVER

Chapter Nine _____

'YES, I'M A crone, I suppose,' said Mama Zep. 'That's what people call after me as I walk down the street. Usually the men. "You old crone!" they scream. "You damn old crone!" But it's a compliment, you know. All my life I've wanted to be a crone. It should be the ambition of everyone. You see, what is a crone? A crone is someone who sits and thinks. Someone who has seen it all, done everything, knows all there is to know, and now sits in a rocking-chair and thinks about it all. And the rocking-chair is important as well. Rocking backwards and forwards. Rocking and thinking. Thinking and rocking. Tick-tock, tick-tock.

'That's why people are scared of crones. They know too much. In particular, a crone scares men. That's why they used to burn them as witches. Oh, yes, a few hundred years ago I would have been tied to the stake and burnt as a witch, of that I have no doubt. For what? For being a crone. Yes, men want to destroy crones. Crones: the wise old women who can see right through them, see right through them as if they were made of glass. Years ago they could legally kill us. Now they can't. So they try other ways. What do they do? They scream "You old crone!" after us. They can't stone me to death any more. But they can try to stone me with words. Oh, sticks and stones, sticks and stones.

'I always thought you had to be old in order to be a crone. That was until Petra Gerda came along. You see, she taught me otherwise.

Some children are born with the knowledge inside them. They are born old and wise. Petra Gerda was one such person. I knew it as soon as I spoke to her. As soon as I saw her I knew. I knew her for what she was. She was already a crone. And that's why people were afraid of her. They were afraid of her power.'

'Was she born around here?' I asked.

'No. Well, that's to say she was born a couple of miles away. You know what it's like around here. It's a cluster of little villages. More so years ago, of course. But it still goes on today. So she was born a couple of miles away. But that might as well have been on another planet for all anyone knew about her in this street. Rachel Sims got to be her friend. But Rachel already had a best friend.' She smiled. 'Rachel had been best friends with someone for as long as she had been alive.'

She waited.

'My mother,' I said.

'Oh, yes. Your mother, Connie Webster. Your mother. Rachel Sims and Faith Niven. They were always together. Playing. They grew up together, dressed in the same way, laughed at the same things. And they were both so beautiful together. So very beautiful. They did some shopping for me now and then when I was too ill to leave the house. And, in return, I would conjure images for them in my crystal ball.'

'You can do that?'

'I used to be able to. Quite easily. It's not so easy for me any more.'

'So?'

'Well, Petra Gerda loved all this. She was already a wizard, you see.'

'She had magic?'

'Oh, not in the same way as Judge Martin. But, yes, there was a kind of magic there. She couldn't crack cups or turn milk sour or see ghosts. But, yes, she was magic alright. But, in her case, the magic was part of her. No, something separate. But part of her soul. In a way, she was the magic herself.'

'There's something I've got to ask,' I said, taking the letter and photograph from my pocket. 'I found these in my mum's bedroom. I have to find out.' I gave them to her.

She glanced briefly at the photograph. Then read the letter. She nodded and smiled.

'Yes,' she said. 'I thought so.'

'Were Rachel Sims and my mother lovers? Is that why my mother hated Judge Martin so much? Because he took Rachel from her?'

Mama Zep gave me back the letter. She studied my face carefully. There was a distressed look in her eyes.

'Oh, Concord Webster,' she said. 'Who can ever say what our feelings are? Sometimes they destroy us and we don't even know it. Although, what you've said, about Rachel and your mother, is slightly true.'

She pointed at the photograph. 'This is your mother. She's hardly changed. As beautiful now as she was then. This is Rachel Sims here.'

'So this one . . .' I began.

'Petra,' said Mama Zep. 'Yes. Petra Gerda.'

'And through the window?'

'My beautiful Judge Martin. You see what a good-looking boy he was. Oh, his eyes were so black. And his lips so red. His looks worked against him, I suppose. His wonderful looks. Everything was against him right from the start. He never stood a chance.' She thrust the photograph back into my lap. 'Oh, this is going to be so complicated. So many stories going on at once. Where? Where?'

'Just talk,' I said.

'But it's not enough. Telling it will never be enough. How can I ever make you understand what came after if I can't make you see what happened before. I must try to tell it to you so that you will understand. The story is such a dark one. So very dark.' She sighed and looked out of the window. 'Look at all these houses. You know the people inside them. Smile at them. They say hello. But inside . . . Oh, the houses are nothing but cages and the people are demons with human masks. Nothing more. Snakes inside. One scream is all it takes you know. Just one scream will make the gorgon open her eyes and turn this home-loving street into a lynch mob. Oh, the ignorance. God help me. The ignorance.'

She walked over to the table and touched the crystal ball.

'I pray for another ending,' she said. 'If I could go back and change things I would. They could have all been so happy. There was no reason for it all to end the way it did. It didn't have to be that way. Things could have been so different.'

'Different. How?'

'The street must change. Oh, the street is a living thing. Organic. Don't ever underestimate it. The street lives and breathes and controls. In the summer the brickwork burns and sweats, in the winter it shivers and shakes. It is part of the people. The people worship the brick of the street. And the brick of the street is ignorance.'

She took a doll from the shelf and cradled it in her arms. Then she sat opposite me again.

'I told you that this is the story of three. Of three girls. But it's really the story of three girls and two men. So, while they cremate one of the two men, let me tell you about him. Judge.'

'Judge Martin the magical,' I said.

'The magical. At first. Yes. Without doubt. But, as surely as craters crawl on the moon, if we suppress that magic it turns black and corrupt inside us and makes monsters of us all. Monsters of helplessness, I suppose.'

'Is that what happened to Judge Martin?'

'I believe so, yes.' She kissed the doll. 'Yes. Let's start. There was once a boy named Steven Feather. I didn't know him that much. But, well, I knew him by sight. He was like a little blackbird. Double-jointed and agile. Judge Martin and Steven Feather were in love.'

She paused for a while. Her lipless mouth twitched.

'Their relationship was a secret,' she said. 'I found out about it later. But, at that time, Judge Martin only told one person about it. He told his best friend. He told the only person he trusted in the whole world.' And she looked at me.

'My mother,' I whispered.

'Yes. He told Faith Niven. Your future mother.'

'My mum and Judge were friends?'

'The best of friends.'

'But Rachel was . . .'

'Well, you can have more than one best friend, I suppose. But, again, it's not as simple as that. Judge Martin saw Faith as his best friend, Faith saw Rachel as her best friend, and Rachel . . .'

'Who was going to marry Judge?'

'Oh, yes. The triangle, you see. Rachel was always going to marry Judge. It was one of those ordained things. Fate, if you like. People pretend that arranged marriages don't go on around here, but they're wrong. They go on all the time. It was always said that Rachel and Judge were to be married. And this suited Faith Niven fine. You see, she just wanted Rachel to be near her. They had arranged it all. They would both get married, live in the same street and – although they had their respective husbands – they would always be together.'

'So are you trying to say . . .?'

'Mmm?'

'My mother was in love with Rachel?'

'Oh, yes. That's true. In a way.'

'But . . .'

'You must understand this much, Connie Webster. Whatever your mother is to do next in this story, she did solely to keep Rachel near her. Heaven knows, I've tried to understand the ins and outs of it all.

I've thought about it and thought about it, old crone that I am. All these years I've been thinking about it. And it still makes no sense. Well, perhaps not *no* sense. Because it does make some kind of sense. In a way. In the way of feelings.

'You see, Rachel and your mother had it all worked out. Rachel, as you know, would marry Judge. Your mother would marry Ronnie, although your father wasn't even around when all these plans were being made. And they would live happily ever after. I think they both saw their future as one unremitting hell. But – as far as your mother was concerned at least – she could put up with this hell so long as Rachel suffered it with her. Does that make sense to you?'

'Yes,' I said. 'I'm afraid it does.'

'I thought it might.'

'But were Rachel and my mother . . .?'

'Lovers?'

'Yes.'

'Did they sleep together? You know, I'm still not sure. I don't think so. You see, at that time, here . . . No. I'm sure they did not. That's what caused all the trouble. Their love could have been, but yet they concealed it. The street made them do it. And so they made masks and their faces grew ugly beneath their masks. At least, that's what happened to your mother. It wasn't quite so bad for Rachel. Mainly because she did care for Judge. Yes, she did love him.'

'But I was always told . . .'

'What?'

'That she hated him. That he used to beat her and torture her. That he was a . . .'

'A devil?'

'Yes.'

'Who told you these things?'

'Well, the whole street knows.'

'But who started them all, do you think?'

'My mother,' I said, softly.

'Yes. Your mother. Let me tell you something, Connie Webster. Once and for all. Judge Martin was no monster, no devil. He was an angel. A magical angel. And your mother took that magic from him and tortured him with it.'

I stared at her blankly.

'Carry on,' I said.

'Let me think. Yes. Everything was going just fine. For your mother that is. The wedding was planned, Jessica Silver was dying. Yes. Everything was as your mother wanted it. Until . . .'

'Steven Feather?'

'Exactly. Until Judge Martin fell in love with Steven Feather. I believe we have only one chance of happiness, Connie Webster. The more I see, the more I believe that. In each of our lives we are destined to meet our one great love. The one person who will make sense of everything. Most people miss their chance and spend the rest of their lives in the wilderness. But a few of us – the lucky ones – recognize that person and hold them. Hold them tight. Yes. Steven Feather was Judge Martin's one chance of happiness.'

'Where did he meet him?'

'I don't know. I knew very little about the whole thing. But, oh, Steven was a marvellous young man. Small, as I say. Like a little blackbird or starling. He would perch on his seat like a bird. He would sit, where you're sitting now, and laugh and giggle. Even in his late teens – as he was then – he had a laugh like a baby. And he was a born ventriloquist. He could throw his voice to the other side of the room and make my dolls talk to me. Oh, Steven. I loved Steven like my own son. You couldn't help but fall in love with him. He was a born mimic as well. He could impersonate anyone. Oh, Steven, Steven. But, you see, he is just a sub-plot. He had nothing to do with the eventual – what shall I say? – tragedy, if you like. And yet, in a way, he was the beginning of it all. Because of what your mother did. What she did to Steven and Judge. Because of what she did to my little Steven Feather, she had a lesson in spite. A lesson in deceit. It was a lesson she was to put to perfect use later on.

'You see, your mother knew that in order to keep Rachel near her it was necessary for Rachel to marry Judge.'

'So?'

'Oh, but Judge was planning to run away, you see. Run away with Steven Feather.'

'But, then, surely my mum would simply have Rachel all to herself.'

'No,' said Mama Zep. 'Because, as your mother knew, if Rachel was under no obligation to marry Judge she would go to the person who she was really in love with. She would go to her own one chance of happiness.' And she smiled and waited.

'Petra Gerda,' I said.

'Yes. Petra Gerda.'

'But it doesn't make any sense,' I said.

'Of course it doesn't. That's what makes it real. Feelings, you see. There was no logic, no reason. Just feelings. And they were all so young. So young and new. They had no experience. There was just passion, jealousy, obsession, possession, need, want. Just feelings. It could have all been so different. But it wasn't. You see, Judge could have been with Steven, Petra could have been with Rachel. It could have all been so easy.'

'But my mother?'

'Ahh. Exactly. Your mother. You see, there was no place for Faith Niven in this perfect world.'

'So what happened? What did she do?'

'For years I've been trying to piece it all together. It's so complicated. Feelings, again, feelings. There is no logic. You see, she had to make sure Rachel married Judge.'

'Yes?'

'That meant getting Judge away from Steven.'

'Yes?'

'So she told Steven's parents about the relationship. To say that all hell broke loose is an understatement. Oh, God, poor Steven. He was helpless. His father beat him to an inch of his life. I remember it all so well. His father dragged him down the street, hitting him with a leather belt. And people just watched from the windows and did nothing. His family locked him in a cupboard. They treated him like an animal.'

I thought for a while, then said:

'That photograph I found . . .'

'Yes. The three girls together. I thought you'd come back to that. What you're thinking is right. Steven took that photograph. It's his shadow you see on the pavement. A few days before Judge and Steven were due to elope Judge got Steven to take that photograph. You see, he loved them all. In a way. He cared for them. He wanted to have the photograph as a keepsake. So he wouldn't forget them. But he made one mistake.'

'He told Faith Niven his plans.'

'Yes.'

'So what happened?'

'Steven's parents never told anyone how they found out. And no one suspected Faith. Least of all Judge, her best friend. Oh, she was a clever one. A real snake in the grass. She was the attitude of the street incarnate.'

'So it was over between them.'

'Well, Steven ran away. The proverbial tied sheets from his bed-room window. He ran away. And that left . . .'

'Judge.'

'Judge. Yes. Oh, I can just imagine how your mother handled all this. To put it in a nutshell, though, he married Rachel, she got pregnant, and your mother married Ronnie, and everything was as your mother wanted it. Until Petra Gerda.'

'But she had always been there?'

'Oh, yes. But she was a crone, you see. A born crone. She went away for a while. After Rachel was married. I think she lost all hope of ever having Rachel. Too much was against her. Although she never suspected your mother. None of us did. And so she went away. But she came back. She came back determined to save Rachel.'

I looked at the clock on the wall.

'I'll have to go soon,' I said.

'Well, that's a good place to leave it,' she said. 'We're at the final stage now.'

'The letter, though?'

'Yes?'

'It was to my mum.'

'No. It was to Rachel. Petra gave it to your mum to give to Rachel. But Rachel never got it. I didn't know of its existence until you showed it to me. But it makes sense now.'

I stood up.

The day was a golden yellow outside. Bird-song filtered in through the half-open window.

'You still miss him, don't you,' I said.

'Who?'

'Steven Feather.'

'Oh, yes. I still miss him. I dream about him, though. So he isn't gone for good.'

'What happened to him?'

'I don't know. Other places. They find other places. It's best forgotten, I believe. It was all such a waste.'

As she showed me to the door she said;

'He's here. You know that.'

'Who?'
'The son. Cromwell.'
'Oh, yes. I saw him.'
'He looks just like his father.'
'Yes.'
She grabbed my arm.
'Oh, redemption, Concord Webster. Redemption!'
And closed the door.

Chapter Ten _____

AS I WALKED into the shop Dicky Tallis was just leaving. He had his bright mauve Edwardian jacket on and his hair was greased into an impeccable quiff. Albeit streaked with grey.

'Hello,' I said.

He looked straight through me.

'Don't forget the lights when you close up,' he called to Lover-boy.

'No,' said Tal. 'I'll try not to.'

'Don't try. Do it.'

'Hello,' I said again.

'Concord,' he said curtly. And left.

'Sorry about that,' said Tal.

'I don't believe it. Your dad's not talking to me because he's had an argument with my dad.'

'Well, your dad walked straight past me as well.'

'It's incredible. After all these years. It just doesn't make any sense.'

'Mum says they're acting like babies.'

'Well, they are. How long can this go on?'

'For ever, dad says.'

'Oh, it's too stupid for words. Really. Your mum can't talk to my mum, I can't talk to you. What was the fight over anyway?'

'No one seems to know.'

'Hasn't your dad said anything?'

'No. Has yours?'

'No. Not a dicky-bird.'

'Look. I don't think you should come here. Not until it dies down a little bit. Yes? I mean it only puts my dad in a bad mood and then he takes it out on me. Or mum. Which is even worse. Yes? What do you say?'

'You mean we shouldn't see each other?'

'Oh, no, Con. Don't be silly. Not that. But perhaps we should only see each other in the Castle for the time being. Until it all blows over.'

'How long will that take?'

'Not long. You know how these things are.'

'Yes. And this could last for ever. Your dad says so.'

'Nothing lasts for ever,' said Tal.

'Some things do. That's the problem.'

I sat on my bed and looked at the photograph. There they were. The three girls.

This is the story of threes.

Rachel stood in the middle of the three girls, Petra to the left; both girls were staring at the camera, smiling. My mother stood to the right, she was looking at Rachel. From the bottom centre of the photograph there rose a shadow, Steven Feather's shadow, it cut at an angle across the photograph to rest on my mother. In the background, to the left, there was a window. Behind this window was the blurred face of Judge Martin. He was looking directly at the camera. I studied the photograph closely. Yes. Now I knew what that look was. Judge Martin was looking at me with love in his eyes.

'Give them to me!'

I turned. Mum stood behind me. She had a face-pack on. It looked like a death-mask.

'Give them to me!' she said.

I handed them to her.

'How dare you take my things!'

'I know about . . .'

'I don't give a fuck what you know about. Do you hear me? I just don't give a fuck. I didn't bring you into the world to judge me. I don't care what stories Mama Zep is telling you. I just don't care. It's not your place to judge me. You don't know anything. How can you? How can you know what I felt. Feel. And Mama Zep will never know. Despite all her stories.'

It was the most animated she had been since Judge Martin's death. Her eyes blazed. At that moment – I know – she hated me. I could feel it. And I hated her too. I wanted to hurt her. More than anything I wanted to make her suffer.

'She told me about Steven Feather,' I said.

She stared at me. Her hands were shaking.

'She doesn't know anything,' she snarled.

'She knows enough.'

'Enough is not everything.'

'I know what you did.'

'I'm not going to let you judge me, Connie. You have no right to do that. Not after all I've done for you. Not after everything I've sacrificed.'

'What have you sacrificed?'

'Things.'

'What things?'

'Oh, God. How can you talk to me like this? I don't care what she tells you. I did what I had to do. To stay alive. To want to stay alive. You can't understand this. No one will ever understand. I . . . needed to . . . to love . . .'

'You love. And Rachel dies,' I said.

Hurt her, said my mind. Make her bleed.

'You don't have to tell me that. I know Rachel died. I was there. I was there when she died.' And she was crying now. Tears cut dark lines through her cracked face-pack. 'I saw her die. I watched her give up. I was there when Cromwell was born.'

'He's here again.'

'So I've heard.'

'Have you seen him?'

'No.'

'Do you want to?'

'Not particularly.'

I pushed past her and rushed down the stairs.

'Connie!' she called after me. 'Wait!'

'What?'

'I'm not . . . I'm not the only guilty one. We were all as guilty as each other. You must see that.'

'What about Steven Feather? Was he guilty of anything?'

'But he had nothing to do with it. Not really.'

'Exactly,' I said.

And slammed the door.

'I suppose,' said Loverboy, opening a can of lager and throwing himself on to the sofa beside me, 'we won't be having a birthday party for me this year. What with all the trouble.'

'No,' I said. 'Suppose not.'

'That'll be the first one we miss.'

'Yes.'

I studied the surrealist room that was our hideaway. I felt at home here. It was where I belonged. The world outside was destroying me. Only in the Castle was I safe. It was a kind of sanctuary.

'I've got something to show you,' said Tal.

'What?'

'Promise you won't tell anyone.'

'Not if you don't want me to.'

He put his hand in his pocket and took out a small black box. Inside there was a beautiful diamond and ruby ring.

'It's for Angel,' he said. 'Her engagement ring.'

'Oh.'

'We plan to be married by the end of the summer.'

'Oh?'

'It's a nice ring. Yes?'

'Very.'

'I thought I had to get one. God knows, everyone's been giving enough hints. And Angel's been so fed up lately.'

'So you think you would just up and marry her and end all her troubles.'

'Now why are you giving me a hard time? I thought you'd be pleased.'

'I am pleased, Tal. If it's what you both want. I am. Really.'

'Well, it is. What we want.'

'Then congratulations.'

'And you'll be best man and we'll all be together. You can move in with Angel and me when we get our own place. Yes? Would you like that? Yes?'

I couldn't speak.

'Yes?' he asked.

I nodded.

'It will still be the three of us together. For ever,' said Tal. 'I can stand it just so long as you're with me. You won't ever leave me, will you, Con?'

I shook my head.

'And you'll always be my friend?'

'Yes,' I said.

And I stared at the skull in the television set.

★

The next morning mum was up early and had cooked breakfast by the time I got down.

'There's scrambled eggs on toast if you want it,' she said. 'If you don't want it you can just throw it away.'

'I'll have it.'

'Tea?'

'Okay.'

'Call your father.'

'I'm here, I'm here,' said dad, strolling into the kitchen. 'No time for anything. I'm late as it is. Bye.' And he left.

The door slammed.

'He'll break a window one day,' said mum. 'What are you up to today?'

'I don't know.'

'More stories?'

'I don't know. But that's a possibility.'

'I see.' She sipped her tea. 'I can't fight you on this, Con. I'm not going to let you drag me down. Not now. I just won't let it happen. I'm stronger than you think. And I've suffered enough. Do you hear me? Enough. God! You don't know. You think it's been easy? I won't be dragged down. Not by my own son.'

I stared in her eyes.

'You made others suffer,' I said.

'But they're all dead now.'

'Dead?'

'Yes. They're the lucky ones.'

'All of them. Petra dead?'

'Yes. Petra. Oh, she hasn't told you that yet, then. Yes. Petra's gone as well.'

'How?'

'I don't know.'

I stood up and put my cutlery in the sink.

'Did you hate Petra?' I asked.

'No.'

'Did you hate Judge?'

'Oh, no.'

'Then why?'

She stood up and pushed past me. She started doing the washing up.

'Don't ask me,' she said. 'Don't ask me anything any more. I don't want to tell you. You have no right to know. It's not my story.'

'Then whose is it?'

She looked at me and smiled.

'Yours by the looks of things,' she said.

I was walking down the street when a pigeon flew past me. So close it almost touched my cheek. I watched it circle up, black against the blue sky, then down, past my cheek again, and then land. Land on the shoulder of Cromwell Martin.

He was dressed in black shirt, black jeans and a bright red kerchief round his neck.

'It loves me I think,' he said. 'I've had it for ages. No matter how hard I try to get rid of it, it still comes back to me. Watch this.' He took the bird from his shoulder and threw it into the air. The pigeon exploded in a frenzy of feathers, then flew back to him. Cromwell ducked out of the way, ran, tried everything he could to elude the bird, but it still sought him and landed on his shoulder again. 'There. You see,' he said. 'Is that love do you think?'

'Of a kind,' I said.

'Yes. Just of a kind. Is it a good kind, do you think?'

'The bird seems to think so.'

'She does, doesn't she.'

'What about you?'

'Oh, I don't know. Sometimes I could kill her. Although I don't

know what I'd do without her. Is it better to love or be loved, do
you think? My name's Cromwell Martin.'

'I know. I'm sorry about your father.'

'No need. I didn't know him. I only ever saw him once or twice
when he came to visit us. I think he was afraid of me.'

'You think so?'

'Well, I don't know. We never know our parents, do we. We
only ever get to know their . . . their shadows.'

'Or masks,' I said.

'Yes. Exactly. What's your name?'

'Connie Webster,' I said.

'Oh, yes. My aunt told me about you. You did some shopping for
her.'

'That's right.'

'She seems to think we were made for each other.'

'Funny,' I said. 'I was just thinking the same thing.'

Helen made us some lunch. She watched us out of the
corner of her eye the whole time. There was a strange look of
contentment over her face as she struggled her way through tea and
sandwiches.

'I'm not used to all this housework,' she said. 'My hands were
made for better things.'

'She's an artist,' said Cromwell.

'Don't use that word in the kitchen, darling,' she said. 'It'll turn
Connie off his food.'

She put some plates in front of us and sat down.

'You should have come to the funeral,' she said. 'It was the most
boring thing I've ever been through.'

'Didn't you love your brother?' I asked.

'No. I couldn't have done. I suppose I must have loved him when
we were children. But, you see, I just loved the farm so much when I

was evacuated there during the war. I was older than Judge, you see. He came after the war so he missed all that. And, then, when I came back all I can remember are bad things. My father was such a monster, you see. He beat me and my mother. All I ever wanted to do was get away. Get back to the farm. Oh, I know I shouldn't blame Judge for all this. But I have such bad memories. And he's just part of them. Simple as that. I never had any desire to come back home. Not once. Oh, I came to mum's funeral, saw Judge and all that. But I didn't come back to the house, the street. And I wouldn't have come back now except that . . .'

'*I* wanted to come back,' said Cromwell.

'Why?' I asked.

'I don't know. It just seemed to make sense.' He fed some crumbs to the pigeon as it sat on his shoulder.

'Must we have Orpheus in here!' exclaimed Helen.

'It's not hurting anyone.'

'It just seems wrong somehow.'

And we all laughed.

'I don't see how you could cut yourself off completely,' I said. 'It doesn't seem possible.'

'Oh, anything's possible. You wait. You'll see. I just wasn't happy here. These things happen. I'm living proof of that. One day you wake up and you think, "I don't need that part of my life any more. It means nothing to me." You see. Easy.'

Coo-coo, said the bird.

'Oh, take him outside,' said Helen.

'It's a girl.'

'A miracle!'

I went up to Cromwell's room. The walls were a dazzling white and the only piece of furniture was the bed. There was a mirror propped up in one corner.

'It's a bit empty,' he said. 'Aunt Helen's cleared everything out.'

'She doesn't waste much time,' I said.

'She's got so much energy. Too much. It's like trying to row an ocean liner talking to her sometimes.'

The bird flew to the window-sill.

'Why call it Orpheus?' I asked.

'My aunt named it. I don't even know who Orpheus was.'

'He went to the Underworld.'

'What for?'

'To save someone he loved, I think.'

'A bit drastic.'

'Perhaps it's necessary sometimes.'

'I hope not.'

'Wouldn't you go into hell to save someone you loved?'

'Depends.'

'On what?'

'On how much I loved them.'

'What about how much they loved you?'

'Oh, that's a different thing altogether.'

'Why?'

'I don't know. It just is.'

We sat on the bed.

'Have I seen you before?' he asked.

'You looked at me from the funeral car.'

'No. I mean before that. Somewhere else.'

'I shouldn't think so.'

'But I feel as if I know you.'

'I feel as if I know you too.'

'But how can that be?'

Coo-coo, said the bird.

'Be quiet, Orpheus,' said Cromwell.

'Magic,' I said.

'What?'

'Feeling we know each other.'

Coo-coo.

'Orpheus,' he said softly.

We kissed.

We stood naked in front of the mirror.

'Look at yourself,' I told him. 'Tell me what you see.'

'Eh?'

'Describe yourself to me.'

'Black hair, shiny black hair combed back, black eyebrows, dark eyes, deep-set eyes, pale complexion, sharp features, bright red lips, broad shoulders, flat stomach.'

'That's what you see.'

'That's what I see.'

He held me. 'What do you see when you look in the mirror,' he asked.

'Us,' I replied.

'Loverboy called to see you,' said mum when I got in. 'He said he wants to see you as soon as possible. Don't tell your father.'

'Why?'

'You know as well as . . .'

'I'm not going to stop seeing Tal because he says so.'

'And you don't want to do anything you don't want to, do you?'

'No,' I said. 'That's right.'

'Oh, all I want is a bit of peace and quiet in this house.'

'Well, you're not going to get it, are you?'

'Not from you I'm not.'

'Damn right you're not.'

She stormed upstairs.

I followed her into her bedroom.

'I met him,' I said.

'Who?'

'Cromwell Martin.'

'Really! Now get out.'

'I'm going to tell him about you.'

'Oh, get out, Connie.'

'He's got a right to know.'

'I said get out.'

'I'm going to tell him exactly what you are.'

Mum jumped on me. She grabbed me round the shirt collar and pushed me against the wall. As she held me there she kicked at my legs. I pushed her away. She pounced on me again and clawed at my face with her nails. I felt them tear through my cheek. She slapped me. Blood dripped from my mouth.

'Stop it!' I screamed. 'Stop it!'

'You bastard!'

'Stop it!'

I kicked at her ankles and grabbed her round the throat. I punched her hard in the stomach.

Finally, we lay sweating and exhausted on the floor. There was blood over my face and on the shirt. Mum's hair was in her eyes and most of her nails were broken.

She started to cry.

'Oh, get out,' she sobbed. 'Just get out.'

'I hate you!' I said.

'Yes.'

'I hate you! I hate you!'

'Get out!' she screamed.

      I was in the bathroom bathing my cuts when dad got home.

'Who did that?' he asked.

'Ask mum,' I said.

'Did she do that?'

'Ask her.'

'What are you doing to her, Con? She's never so much as raised her voice to you before.'

'Ask her. I'm not saying anything.'

'I will.'

'I'm going to see Loverboy in a minute. So I might be late.'

'Now you know what I . . .'

'I don't care, Dad. He's my friend.'

'I don't want you to see him.'

'I'll do what I think is right.'

'But . . .'

'I don't give a fuck, Dad.'

'How dare you! How dare you talk to me like that. It was all because of you that I had a fight with Dicky in the first place.'

I stared at him.

'Because of me. But why?'

'He called you names.'

'What names?'

'He said you were trying to spoil it between Loverboy and Angel.'

'He said what?'

'You heard.'

'So you hit him.'

'Yes. It's a lie.'

'Is it?'

'Isn't it?'

'You're not sure and you still hit him?'

Dad took a step towards me.

'If I ever thought . . .' he began.

'Yes?'

'Nothing.'

'Say it.'

'No. Where's your mother?'

'In her room.'

Dad started to walk up the stairs.

'Loverboy bought Angel's engagement ring today,' I said. 'That should please everyone.'

'I see. That's that then.'

'Yes,' I said. 'That's that.'

  I took my dragon head to the Castle. The mask was finished now. I had decided not to give it eyes. The holes in the mask would be enough. They seemed more real somehow.

I put the mask on and sat watching the skull in the television set.

And I thought, I am in love. For the first time I am in love. And loved. Someone loves me. And I love them. And within me things clicked and whirled like the insides of some gigantic clock, cog against wheel, spring against spiral, tick against tock, and I knew that nothing would ever be the same again. I had shown someone what I really was. I had shown someone my truth, my secret. Out there, beyond the walls of the Castle, there was a boy who had seen inside my chrysalis. And I would never be safe again.

I heard footsteps. Through the holes in the mask I saw Loverboy come down the stairs. He smiled at me and opened a can of lager.

'You look pretty,' he said.

I nodded.

'Lost your voice?'

I shook my head.

'Oh, I'm not in the mood for your games, Connie.' He took a swig from the can. It trickled down his chin. 'Angel liked the ring. Yes? She cried when she saw it. Fancy that. She kissed me and she cried. She acted really surprised as well. As if she didn't expect it. We haven't told Frank and Sheila yet. Might do that tonight. Oh, the fucking ritual of it all. I hate it.'

'Then why do it?'

'What do you mean "why do it"? What choice have I got? What else is there to do?' He peered at me suspiciously. 'What have you been up to today?'

'I met Cromwell Martin.'

'I saw him as well. From a distance, though. He looks a sinister bastard to me.'

'He's okay.'

'He looks like a vampire.'

'Appearances,' I said.

'I wish you'd take that mask off.'

'Why?'

'It bugs me, Connie. That's why.'

'It's just an appearance.'

'Oh, God, you're in one of your aloof arty moods.'

'Not at all.'

'Oh, Jesus!'

I removed the mask. My face was red and sweating. Hair stuck to my forehead.

'What's happened to you?' asked Tal.

'Eh?'

'The scratches on your face.'

'I had an argument with a lamp-post,' I said.

Tal turned away from me.

'What's wrong?' I asked.

'Nothing,' he mumbled.

'You can tell me.'

'Can I?'

'What's that supposed to mean?'

'Oh, nothing.'

I went over to him. We sat on the sofa. I put my arm round his shoulders and he leant against me. His hair smelt of fresh apples.

'I don't understand any of this,' he said.

'No?'

'With Angel, I mean. I wish somebody would tell me what was going on.'

'Do you love her?'

'No.'

'Then why marry her?'

'Because I have to. It's expected. You know that. And what else will I do if I don't marry her? What will she do? No. I have to marry her.'

'But if you don't love her . . .'

'What has that got to do with anything? My mum wants grand-children while she's still young enough to enjoy them. She told me. She can't wait any longer.'

'You're getting married to please your mum!'

He sat up and looked at me.

'Yes,' he said. 'I suppose I am.'

On the way home I called in to see Cromwell.

Helen opened the door.

'Hello, darling,' she said. 'Come into the parlour and all that.'

She had a gin and tonic in one hand.

'Cromwell's upstairs taking a nap. You must have tired him out, lover.'

'Is that a compliment?'

'You bet. Come into the kitchen for a while. I want to talk to you.'

I sat at the table and she poured me a drink.

'I hope you like gin,' she said.

'Fine.'

She sat opposite me and smiled.

'Cromwell has always been a very solitary child,' she said. 'I suppose you can tell that much. He doesn't make friends very easily. But that doesn't mean he's lonely. He's just the solitary type. He's a very vulnerable boy.'

'If you're asking me not to hurt him then I know . . .'

'Oh, I know that, Con. I know you wouldn't do anything to harm him. I can tell that much. No. It's not that at all. You see, I've looked after Cromwell all his life. Judge sent him to me after Rachel died. So I've always thought of him as my own child. Although, heaven knows, I've never had any inclination to have a child of my own. But I took to Cromwell. I loved him at once. Just as you, I believe, loved him at once.'

'I loved him before I knew him,' I said.

'Yes. I believe that. We're always waiting for that special person. You were lucky. You found each other in time. Most of us wait and hesitate. Become deformed.'

'Is that what happened to your brother?'

'I believe it did. I believe he lost everything and then, gradually, simply became what people thought him. They called him a Devil and, in the end, hair grew on his back and . . . Yes. He missed his chance.'

For some reason I was crying.

'Oh, no, Con,' she said, putting her arm round me. 'Don't. It's all over now.'

'I keep seeing him dead. The way he looked. He killed himself. Why did he do it? After all these years?'

'Oh, I don't know. Most suicides take a lifetime.'

'I just wish I could have spoken to him.'

'But you can, you see. You can. You can speak to him through Cromwell. Do you understand? What is lost can be found.'

I wiped my eyes on the cuff of my shirt.

'I want you to spend a week with Cromwell. In our country house. Stay with him there. Love him. Do you understand?'

'Yes,' I said.

'It will be good for both of you. You need to get away just as much as he does.'

I held her hands. The gold rings felt cold and hard. She brought my hand to her lips and kissed each finger in turn.

'He's got his father's eyes, you see,' she said.

I went up to Cromwell's bedroom. He lay asleep in bed. The sheets wrapped tightly around him. I went over to the bed and lay down beside him. As I stared at his face tiny sparks seemed to fly about his head and out, through the half-open window.

Yes, I thought. If each spark is a story, let them fly out. Let the sparks of our story light up the zodiac. Let it be a comet. Let sparks that are stories banish blood on silver for ever.

Chapter Eleven _____

THIS DREAM I remember.

I was dressed as a minstrel and a King was saying to me, 'My child is dying. My beautiful Prince is dying. Only one thing can save him.'

'What?' I ask.

'The Mirror of Truth.'

'And where is the Mirror?' I ask.

'The Mirror is in hell. You must go to hell and find this Mirror for me. Then my son will be saved.'

So I opened a green door and entered hell.

It was dark and foul smelling. Birds attacked me as I entered. Gargoyles tore at my legs.

Pigeons pecked my ears to silence.

'Help!' I screamed.

But could not hear my voice.

Then I found the Mirror. It was being held by the Devil himself. He was combing his black hair.

'So,' said the Devil, 'you have come for the Mirror of Truth.'

I just stared at him.

'Don't you understand that only the Devil can look in the Mirror of Truth and live. It is too much for anyone else to bear.'

'Give it to me!' I screamed.

His breath was hot and sulphurous against my neck, his sharp teeth grazed across my cheek and his talons clawed through my back. As we fought the Devil sucked the eyes from my skull.

I ran from hell.

I was blind and deaf.

But I had the Mirror.

I slammed the green door shut and took the Mirror to the King.

'Here is the Mirror of Truth,' I said to the silent dark. 'This will save your son.'

'It's too late,' said the King. 'The Prince died as your journey began.'

But, of course, I could not hear.

Chapter Twelve _____

'THIS WILL BE the final part of the story,' said Mama
Zep. 'There's not much left to tell. When are you leaving with Cromwell?'

'In the morning,' I said.

'Good. Then I've timed it just right. You'll know what you have
to know before you leave. Oh, this hasn't been an easy story to tell.
No stories are. But this one has been particularly difficult because all
the stories seem to happen at once. It's hard to know where one story
ends and another begins, who the main characters are, which is the
sub-plot, which the main plot. You see, it's the story of how I discovered I had the ability to see ghosts and made my mother cry, it's
the story of Jessica Silver and her changing hair, it's the story of a
child who could crack cups and turn milk sour, it's the story of Judge
Martin and his little Steven Feather, it's the story of how Steven
Feather ran away to start a new life, it's the story of Rachel and her
arranged marriage with Judge, it's the story of your mother and – in
a way – it's also about me, who knew of Judge Martin's magic and
did nothing to nurture it. And, of course, it's about the strongest of
us all. The one who was older than me the day she was born. It's the
story of Petra Gerda.

'Petra Gerda. Ah. The name still has magic. Although Petra's
magic was a special kind. She couldn't crack cups or see ghosts, she
couldn't drive her parents to suicide by telling them secrets. No. Her

magic was herself. Oh, the old crone. The wonderful, wonderful old crone.

'I was called to help at her birth. Oh, I knew the Gerda family vaguely. Although they weren't local they knew who I was. And there was no one else. Oh, I'd never had such a struggle. Never. Cromwell's was a long delivery, but Petra's was worse. You see, she was quite happy where she was. She had already lived a million lives. There was nothing we could teach her. But we still pulled her out. Pulled her out though she struggled to stay there. That's when I saw her lips. They were smooth. No cleft. You see, before we're born we live in a magical cave where all the secrets of life are given to us. As we leave an angel flies down to us and presses its finger against our lips, saying, "Tell no one what you know." It's the pressure of the angel's finger that makes our cleft. But no angel had done this to Petra. That's why she didn't want to be born.

'I knew what I had to do. I had to name the child. So I cleared my mind and held the baby in front of me. She felt as heavy and solid as stone. And then, in the voice of my dead grandfather, I heard her name.

'"Petra," I said.

'And the baby's eyes opened. She reached out and touched my face, leaving a bloody handprint on my cheek.

'When I looked into the baby's eyes I became scared. I knew straight away what she was. A changeling. She looked back at me with eyes older than my own. Eyes so wise and kind I felt like crying.

'And that was how Petra Gerda came into the world.

'Oh, she was different right from the beginning. She didn't want to wear the same clothes as everyone else. She wanted to look different, be different. In a place where everyone tried their best to look and think the same Petra stood out like a sore thumb. Nobody understood her. Least of all her own parents. And what people don't understand they try to destroy. Even as a girl Petra made people feel uncomfortable. Not because she was spiteful or vindictive. On the contrary. There was such love and joy inside her. But, you see, that was the whole problem. She was just too perfect. Too wise.'

'A crone,' I said.

'A crone. A witch. Exactly. People would have burnt her in the Dark Ages. But we're not living in the Dark Ages now. Or so we're told. Petra made people feel uncomfortable because she saw straight through them. As if they were made of glass. She saw them for what they really were. Their souls if you like. And, in most cases, she didn't like what she saw there. Greed, avarice, ignorance. She saw it all. No one fooled her. Except . . .' She hesitated.

'Except?'

'Listen. She was a solitary child. I made her dolls to play with. She would sit in my garden for hours. The garden was beautiful in those days. Not the jungle it is now. And so Petra passed her time. Alone. Though not lonely. She went to school. And she made a friend. Her first really close friend. The first person she felt anything for, I believe.'

'My mother?'

'Yes. You see, it was Faith Niven who first brought Petra into the circle. The circle that included . . .'

'Rachel.'

'Exactly. And so the three girls were at last brought together. The potion was complete. Everything was set in motion.'

'Fate,' I said.

'Exactly. The three girls were together. They were always in each other's company. And then something happened. Something your mother had not foreseen.'

'Petra and Rachel fell in love,' I said.

'Yes,' she said, nodding. 'Petra and Rachel fell in love. They came here, to my house, to make love. Upstairs in my bedroom. It was the only place they could go. The only place they were safe. Oh, they were so perfect. I loved them both. So beautiful. They had everything planned. Or rather Petra did. They would run away, live together. I can still hear Petra's voice now. It was full of such hope.' Tears filled her eyes. 'Oh, Rachel was confused by it all. You see, things like that simply did not happen. She couldn't see it as even remotely possible. Oh, the innocence . . . The ignorance. Petra tried to convince her. Tried to make her see that it was possible. And I think she would have succeeded. Were it not for one person. The one person to fool Petra.'

'Faith Niven.'

'Your mother, yes.' She held my hand. 'Listen to me, Concord Webster, you must not judge. That isn't your place. I'm telling you all this so that you *know*. Just that. There is no time for revenge and recrimination now. All we can do is save what we have. Hold what is possible. Do you understand? It's not important that you think it right or wrong. It's just important that you know.'

'Yes,' I said softly. 'Yes.'

'I want to talk about Judge Martin again. In a way it all centres on this. As I've already told you, Faith told Steven Feather's parents, thus ending it all between the two boys. Oh, they weren't strong, you see. They were trapped into doing what the street thought they had to do. A time and a place has a power over us all. And the street, then as now, had a power. A dark, brooding, insidious energy. Just what torture the poor Steven Feather had to endure I'll never know. Oh, not just physical tortures – though, heaven knows, they were bad enough – but mental torture. Torture of the spirit. The poor, gentle starling. He ran away. Well, at least he *did* something. But Judge had to stay. What else could he do? His mother was ill. She had had a stroke, you see, and needed him with her. He was trapped. Trapped by the street, the house, and his ignorance. Oh, darker still, darker.

'Your mother told Jessica about Judge and Steven. Quite why she did this I'll never understand. She had already achieved her objective. But, whatever her reasons, the rest is easy to understand. Faith told Rachel that Judge needed her, Faith told Judge that Rachel needed him. Oh, on and on. Faith told Petra that Rachel didn't want her. Endless, endless.'

'But it was all lies,' I said. 'Surely someone must have suspected what was going on.'

'Oh, no. Faith was everyone's best friend. It was all so carefully done.'

'And so Judge and Rachel were married.'

'Yes. With Steven gone Judge was powerless. He thought he was doing Rachel a favour. You see, he did care for her. Loved her in a way. But not in the same way he loved Steven. Someone had to teach him his love. Show him what was possible. But – there you are – no one did. So he never knew.

'Oh, I remember the screams of Jessica when she found out about her son and Steven. Can you believe it? She screamed. And every window in the street shattered. It's true. I was there. I saw it. Now I remember it. She screamed and her screams shattered every single window.'

'And Petra?'

'Ah, Petra. Well, she believed what Faith told her, you see. She believed that Rachel no longer needed her. And so she left. She went away. One morning she was gone. No goodbyes. Nothing. She disappeared. Except . . .'

'Except?'

'She came back.'

'She returned for Rachel.'

'Yes. About a year later. Rachel was in her ninth month with Cromwell. And Petra came back. If she was powerful before she left, then she was even more powerful now. At last she could see through the one person who had deceived her. She must have been thinking about it all year. So she came back to claim Rachel. She came back like an angel of vengeance.

'It was the day Cromwell was born. Rachel had started her labour. It was early afternoon. I had been summoned to Rachel's house. Faith had married your father by now. But all the men were at work. You know how the street belongs to women and children during the day. Petra came back. And went straight to Faith Niven.

' "You never gave it to her, did you!" says Petra.

' "Get out of here," says Faith. "You're not wanted."

'You see, the day Petra left she gave your mother a letter to give to Rachel. Your mother was the only one she could trust. The letter, as you know, told Rachel that she still loved her, that it was possible for her to run away. It was Rachel's last chance of escape. I didn't know of that letter's existence until you showed me. But it makes things clearer. You see, I can remember Rachel saying, "She was supposed to have written and she didn't. She left without a word. Perhaps she didn't really love me after all."

'The tragedy is that Rachel died still believing that. Petra gave the letter to your mother and that's where it stayed. All these years.'

'It's just all so senseless,' I said.

'It's not important that it makes sense,' snapped Mama Zep angrily. 'What's important is that it *means* something. That it achieves a kind of meaning.'

'Yes,' I said. 'Carry on.'

'Tell me, Concord Webster. Do you believe in demons?'

'How do you mean?'

'In demons. Demons that possess us. Evil things that make us do things. Against our reason.'

'I don't know,' I said.

'Well, I saw demons that day. First your mother became possessed and then they possessed the whole street. You see, it was almost as if they had been waiting for her. Burn, witch, burn. Oh, the looks in the women's eyes when they saw her. They hated her. Burn, witch, burn. You could smell brimstone in the street that day.'

'But what happened? What actually happened?'

She stood up and went over to the table. She picked up a crystal ball and brought it back with her.

'First, let me tell you how much people hated Petra Gerda. Then you might understand. You see, she flouted all convention. She was a crone, a wizard. I keep saying it because it was true. She had the gift for loving. For her it was all so simple. She loved Rachel, Rachel loved her. Judge loved Steven, Steven loved Judge. Why shouldn't that love be? Why couldn't they all live together? Why should they be forced into a hell because people told them it could not be. It was all so simple for her.

'Oh, yes, the street hated her. She was a danger to them, you see. She threatened them. By simply *being* she undermined all their values. Oh, she was simply wonderful. She went to pubs by herself. Which was unheard of. And she hit men if they made some remark to her. Really punched them. Oh, marvellous. One day she stood at the end of the street and screamed, "You're a bunch of ignorant bastards! All of you! Do you hear me? And I'm not afraid of any of you!" And she wasn't. She wasn't afraid of anything or anyone.

'And so she returned. Blazing like fury and twice as strong. She was ready. She could see the truth. And she was back to rescue Rachel.'

'And she went to my mother's house.'

'Yes.'

'And?'

'And the demons were set free.'

'So? What happened?'

'Oh, it started as an argument between Petra and Faith. On the doorstep. Screams, abuse, accusations.'

'The letter.'

'Yes. The letter. A crowd gathered to watch. Of course, they were on your mother's side. Petra was still what she had always been. An outcast, an intruder. I wasn't there when it all started. I was still tearing Cromwell Martin out of his mother. But that will be told later. As I say, I wasn't there when it began. But from what I was told it was your mother who hit Petra first.'

'Hit her?'

'Oh, yes. Knocked her to the ground. Bloodied her nose and mouth in one blow. But Petra got to her feet and continued her accusations. Your mother played to the crowd. It was a hot summer's day and they could smell blood. And your mother was full of demons. She incited the crowd. Oh, the darkness, the darkness. And, one by one, the crowd joined in. First jeering at Petra, calling her names, accusing her. And then your mother – always your mother – threw something. A milk bottle. And the other women joined in. They hurled anything they could find at Petra.'

'They stoned her,' I murmured.

'Yes. They stoned her. She crawled to my street door. The only safe door she knew in the street. And still the objects hit her, cutting her, hurting her. They would have killed her, Concord. I know that much. They would have killed her. But I stopped them.'

'You heard the noise.'

'Well, yes. But I had no idea what was going on. And, anyway, I couldn't leave Rachel. It was a difficult birth. I'd never seen so much blood. Blood everywhere. The whole bed was red. She died with Cromwell still inside her. I called for some scissors and cut him free. He was born kicking and screaming.'

'And you went down to the street.'

'Yes. And there was Petra curled up on my doorstep. The whole street around her like a pack of wolves. Yes. I saved her. I sent them away. Their lust for blood had been sated now. The demons had been exorcized.'

'And? Yes? And?'

'What is there to say? I bathed Petra's wounds. She told me why she had returned. And I had to tell her. That Rachel was dead. Oh, God. We're all so helpless.'

'So she left?'

'She begged me to let her see the child first. So, that night, when everyone was asleep, we crept back into the house and I showed her the baby boy. She kissed him.

' "Cromwell," she said.

'And that's how he got his name.'

'And Judge Martin?'

'Oh, yes. Poor Judge. He had lost everything, you see. Everything. He sent the child to his sister, Helen. Then his mother died. And, for him, in a way, it was all over. Except . . .'

'Yes?'

'Well, you see, if anyone had been innocent in this it was Judge Martin. But your mother had to have a scapegoat. Guilt, you see, guilt. Rachel was dead. She had made friends with Ivy Tallis by now. Guilt, guilt, guilt. She had to have someone to hook all her guilt on, all her darkness, all her sin.'

'Judge,' I said.

'Yes. She spread stories. All the things she wanted to say about herself – but couldn't – she said about Judge Martin. So she called him a monster, a beast . . .'

'A Devil,' I said.

'Yes. He became her own private devil. In the end, I suppose, he became what people believed him.'

'All the time,' I said, 'my mother remained the same. And he changed. He . . . he . . .'

'Reflected her, I suppose.'

'So when I saw him. Dead. That was . . . my . . . my . . . moth–!'

'Don't think of it, Concord.'

'But couldn't you have done something?'

'No. Believe me.'

'But where did Petra go? What happened to her?'

'I'm not saying any more. My part in the story is over. All I will say is this. Even though Rachel was dead, she still loved her. I was in contact with her for a while. And I told her where to find the child.'

'You told her he was with Helen?'

'Yes.'

'So did she go to Helen?'

'That you will have to ask others.'

I nodded.

'Yes,' I said. 'I see.'

I got up and walked towards the door.

She followed.

As I opened the door she touched my arm.

'Concord,' she said, 'if I told you not to trust Loverboy what would you say?'

'That you're wrong. He's my best friend.'

She nodded and smiled.

'At least I've said it,' she said. 'There's still a chance.'

And closed the door.

Chapter Thirteen _____

WHEN I GOT home Angel was waiting for me. We went
up to my room. She showed me the engagement ring.

'Have you bloody well seen this?' she asked.

'Yes,' I said.

'And what do you think?'

'It's very nice.'

'Oh, very nice. Very nice. Bloody hell. What am I supposed to do
with this thing, eh? Put it through my nose so he can haul me around
like a pig?'

'He thought it's what you wanted.'

'Why is everyone so intent on telling me what I want all the time.
Is this supposed to answer all my problems?'

'I don't know,' I said.

'No. You don't know. And I don't know. And so it goes on. Oh,
yes. This will cure everything. A golden ring. Now I'll be Mrs
Loverboy Tallis and everything will be alright.'

'What do you want then?'

'I don't know what I bloody well want. Can't I just be me without
having to want something all the time? Do I want this? Do I want
that? I don't *know*.' And she hurled the ring at me.

It caught my eye. I yelled in pain and clutched the side of my face.
The ring fell to the carpet.

'Oh, Con.' She held me. 'I'm sorry. Are you okay? Let me see.'

'It's fine,' I said. 'No damage.'

'Let me see.'

I tried to open my eye. But it was sore and watering badly. I sat on the bed.

She fell down beside me.

'Oh, God,' she sighed. 'What a mess.'

'Yes,' I agreed.

'What am I going to do, Con?'

'Tell him.'

'Tell him what?'

'That you don't want to marry him.'

'But how can I? After all this time. And he's just so bloody nice. So pleasant. So considerate. So bloody boring. He's always so amazed by everything. All his little chirping, "Yes? Yes?" '

I folded a tissue, breathed on it and pressed it against my eye.

'If you feel like this . . .' I began.

'Yes?'

'You can't marry him.'

'But what else can I do? Stay at home? Look after Paul all the bloody time? His wheezing drives me even more mad than Lover-boy.'

'So what do you want?'

'Want! You know, Con. I've got this nervous feeling in the pit of my stomach. Like something is about to happen. Something bad. I don't know what it is. But the suspense is killing me.' She picked up the ring and put it on again. 'Jesus! You know why he's so intent on marrying me, don't you.'

'Why?'

'So he can be near you.'

'Oh, that's ridiculous.'

'It's true. He's told me. We'll get married and you'll come to live with us. You see what a child he is.'

'That's all crap. You know that.'

'I know that. You know that. But does he know that?'

'I mean, I love Loverboy. I've always loved him. But I don't love Loverboy like I . . . well . . . you know.'

'Do me a favour, Con. Tell him that. He won't believe it from me.'

'Yes,' I said.

She looked at me and frowned.

'You were about to say something else, weren't you.'

'When?'

'Just now. You said "I don't love Loverboy like I . . ." And you were going to say a name. Someone who you *do* love like that.'

'Yes,' I said.

'Who?'

'Cromwell Martin.'

'And he loves you?'

'Yes.'

'You sound convinced.'

'I am.'

'Then you're lucky. Some of us are left wondering.' She smiled. 'Look. Don't tell Loverboy about you and Cromwell. Not yet anyway. He's liable to do anything.'

'How do you mean?'

'I'm not sure. Sometimes people do the impossible.'

'Not Loverboy.'

'He's a wounded animal, Con. How's your eye?'

'I'll live.'

'Yes,' she said. 'I suppose you will.'

At dinner that night mum said, 'I'm glad you thought it was necessary to ask me if you could go away with a total stranger.'

'I asked dad,' I said.

My dad nodded.

'Yes,' he said. 'It'll do him good. Anything to get him out of this madhouse for a while.'

'What's that supposed to mean?' snapped mum.

'Oh, give it a rest.'

'Is it my fault we treat each other like this?'

'For God's sake.'

'So it's all my fault, eh?'

'I said I don't want to hear any more.'

'Well, you're going to hear some more whether you like it or not, Ronnie Webster.'

'Shut it, woman!'

'It's my house as well as yours. I'll say what I like.'

'I warn you . . .'

'Yes?'

'Shut it!'

'What will you do if I don't?'

'Faith.'

'Hit me, then. Go on. Hit me. Show your son what a man you are. Hit me.'

Dad stood up and threw his plate against the wall.

'For fuck's sake!' he cried.

And stormed out of the house, saying, 'I'm going to the pub.'

We both sat in silence for a while.

'Well,' said mum.

'I know about it,' I said, softly.

'About what?'

'It! Everything. Mama Zep told me.'

Mum put down her knife and fork.

'Oh,' she said. 'I see.'

'Everything. The letter, the lies, Petra Gerda, Steven Feather.'

Mum buried her face in her hands and sighed. She rubbed her eyes and looked at me.

'You think it's all so easy, don't you. Oh, God. Just to think. After all these years I've got to sit here and be judged by you.'

'Is what she told me true?'

'I don't know. Yes, I suppose so. There's no reason for her to lie. But there's as many versions of a story as there are people in it, Connie.'

I stood up and glared down at her.

'You're a witch,' I said.

She flinched.

'An evil witch.'

She flinched again.

'A fucking evil witch,' I screamed. 'I don't want you to be my mother. I don't need you any more.'

'You can't talk to me like that!' she screamed, jumping to her feet. 'I won't allow it. I'm your mother whether you like it or not.'

'I know,' I said. 'And that's *all* you are.'

I left the house.

I took Cromwell to see the Castle.

'Loverboy and I built this room,' I said. 'It's taken us years. Most of our lives. It looks weird doesn't it?'

'Yes,' he said.

'It makes sense to us, though. Everything in here has got its own little story to tell.'

Cromwell sat down.

'This is nice,' he said, touching the blue dolphin.

'A present from Loverboy.'

'It's beautiful.'

'Yes. Sometimes when I look into it I can see other things. Faces and places.'

'A kind of crystal ball.'

'In a way. I had to bring you here. It was important you see it.

With your own eyes. It's important that you know everything there is to know about me. I have to tell you what I am. I want to tell you everything I've ever dreamed. Or wanted to dream.'

He smiled.

Orpheus flew around the room and came to rest on the dragon's head.

'Did you make that?' he asked.

'Yes. It's a mask.'

'Can I try it on?'

'If you like.'

He put the mask over his face.

'Oh, the eyes are just holes,' he said. 'They look real from a distance.'

'Yes. I'm going to boil some water. Would you like a cup of tea?'

'Please.'

I went to a dark corner.

As I filled the kettle I heard footsteps. Looking up I saw Loverboy come into the Castle. He looked at the figure with the dragon's mask on.

'I want to talk to you, Con,' he said. And walked up to Cromwell. He sat opposite him. 'I just don't know what's going on.'

The dragon looked at him.

'I don't know. It's as if everything's falling to pieces. You know what I mean? Yes?'

I came out of the shadows.

'Yes,' I said.

Loverboy jumped to his feet as if I was a ghost.

'Who? You! Then who?' He looked at Cromwell. 'I thought . . .'

I laughed and walked over to him.

'This is Cromwell Martin,' I said.

Cromwell took the mask off.

'Hello,' he said, and held out his hand.

'But . . . but . . .' stammered Loverboy.

'But what?' I asked.

'This is our place.'

'Oh, Tal . . .'

'It is. We've never brought anyone else here before. This is our secret place. That's what we always said. You agreed.'

'Tal, don't be silly. Cromwell and I are . . .'

'I don't want to know.'

'Tal!'

'You bastard!'

He pushed me. I fell to the floor.

'I hate you!' he screamed. 'You've let me down as well.' He picked up the blue dolphin and threw it at me. I avoided it just in time. It shattered in a million pieces across the floor. 'You're a fucking two-faced bastard!'

And he ran out of the Castle.

'I'm sorry,' I said to Cromwell.

'I wonder what got into him.'

'Jealousy.'

'Demons.'

'Exactly.'

'I might well join you by the end of the week,' said Helen. 'I need to get back there.'

We nodded.

Helen looked at us.

'What's wrong?' she asked.

I told her about Loverboy.

'Ah,' she said, nodding. 'I see. It's scared you, has it?'

'Yes,' I said.

'You've seen a side of him you never thought existed. Oh, well. It's something you have to get used to. We can be many people all at the same time.'

'But Loverboy . . .'

'You're trying to understand feelings, Connie. No way. Words are useless. One day I watched a flock of sparrows. There they were. All happily pecking at the breadcrumbs. And then, all of a sudden, they all started to attack one little sparrow. One of their own flock. All of them at the same time. As if a magical signal had been given. I tried to help the bird. It was half-dead. Pecked to a bloody mess. Well, I kept it in my house until it was well. And then I let it go again. No sooner had I let it out than – out of nowhere – the sparrows descended and attacked it again. I wasn't fast enough this time. By the time I got to it the bird was dead. Now. Explain that.'

'I can't,' I replied.

'No. Try not to think about things too much. That's always a danger. Learn to feel things. Just trust what you feel.'

I held Cromwell's hand.

'Look on next week as a journey towards something,' she said. 'Discovering people.'

'Who?' I asked.

'Each other,' she said. 'Perhaps you might even meet a third.'

I frowned.

'A third?'

'Isn't there always a third?' said Helen. 'Casting a shadow?'

'Yes,' I said.

'Then find it,' she said.

When I got home the front door was open. My dad was just leaving. He poked me in the chest when he saw me.

'It's *your* fault,' he said. 'I don't know what's wrong with her. But you're driving her mad. I know that much. And I want it to stop. Do you hear me? I want it to stop!'

He pushed past me and out of the house.

Mum was in the garden. Or rather, what was left of the garden. She had hacked down everything, pulled things up by the roots. Everything was destroyed.

'That's what I think of it,' she said to me. 'You see.' Her hands were covered in blood. She was breathing deeply. 'It's all gone now. That's what I think of your garden.'

She went into the kitchen and started to wash her hands.

'Judge me,' she mumbled. 'After all I've done. I don't care. It's nothing to me. Do you hear me? Nothing. You don't know. How I suffered. You think it was easy for me?' She wiped her hands on a towel. 'If I had known then what I do now . . . Do you think I wouldn't change it if I could? Do you think I'm the only guilty one? Do you?'

She went upstairs without waiting for my reply.

I smelt crushed flowers.

The next morning, before meeting Cromwell, I called in to see Mama Zep.

I told her about mum.

'Yes,' she said. 'Yes.'

'Is that all you're going to say?'

'What else can I say?'

I sighed and sat down.

'Cromwell and I are leaving this morning. We'll be gone about a week.'

'I heard.'

My mind was on mum.

'You know,' I said. 'I think she just wants to meet them again. Just meet them all and say things.'

'What things?'

I shrugged.

'I don't know,' I said. 'Sorry, I suppose.'

'You know something,' said Mama Zep. 'I believe that if we want to meet someone with all our heart, then we will meet them. And if we lose them, meet them again.'

Part Four

In the Eyes of
Mister Fury

Chapter Fourteen _____

WHEN WE ARE born we are magic. We come into the world still sparkling and blind with the secrets whispered to us by a zodiac of blood. Inside the womb blood cells swim in and out of our eyes like tiny comets, giving us stories, the legends of things, names, and when we push our way out of our sacred bubble we are already wizards. We cry, not in pain or fear, but in wonder of all the miracles we might have to perform. And the greatest of all these miracles, the most potent of all magic, is love.

When we are born we have the capacity to love. To love and be loved. Conceived in love, we breathe love as we once breathed blood. This love shimmers round our head like a halo of tadpoles. This love goes into our eyes, clears sight, travels to the mind, gives knowledge, protects us, surrounds us. We are confident and safe in the knowledge that our pilgrimage has already begun. All magic, by its mere nature, seeks other magic. And so our life becomes a journey in which to end loneliness.

When we are born we are all wonderful. But, gradually, masks and streets are erected around us, walls and lies fence us in, make us prisoners, trap us inside our skulls, turn hearts to stone, until the magic – once bright and sparkling – turns black and blistered in our minds. We begin to feel useless and deformed, bitter with unused potential, our magic alienates us, makes us outcasts, intruders, angels become gargoyles. Finally, we shrink into ourselves, fall away, forever broken, denying magic, denying wonder, helpless.

When we are born we are magical and loving and full of wonder. But darkness and ignorance surround us at every corner. Until the day someone calls us a monster or a devil and we believe them.

Chapter Fifteen _____

'TELL ME ABOUT yourself,' I said to Cromwell Martin. 'Speak to me. Tell me things. I want to know everything you've ever done, everyone you've ever known, everywhere you've been. I want to get inside your skull, see what's inside you, feel it with you. I want to know your dreams.'

We lay in bed together. It was our first night in the country house. The window was open and a gentle summer's breeze blew over us.

'My dreams,' said Cromwell.

'Yes. What do you dream? Tell me.'

'When I was a child,' he said. 'I used to have the same dream nearly every night. It wasn't a nightmare. It was a very peaceful dream. It used to give me a kind of strength, I suppose.'

'Tell me,' I said.

'I would be lost in a forest. A beautiful forest. Tall trees full of blossom. All kinds of birds were in the forest with me. Pelicans, seagulls, starlings, blackbirds, sparrows. Although I was lost in this forest I wasn't scared. I felt at home there. It was where I belonged.'

'Tell me some more,' I said. 'Didn't you ever want to see your father?'

'No,' he whispered. 'Not really. I never thought about it. Helen never really mentioned him. And I was happy with her. Does that sound odd?'

'Yes.'

'Well, I suppose it is. I don't know. I've always been so content with Aunt Helen, you see. Oh, what can you say about your own life? You live it and that's it. I grew up, I went to school, I never had any friends. Not really. At school I was always being blamed for things I didn't do. It's because of my looks, I suppose. Sly looks. Sinister. I don't know. I didn't enjoy school very much.'

'Have you always been alone here?'

'Most of the time. There was my aunt's girlfriend. But that was years ago. I don't remember anything about her.'

'When was it?'

'Oh, she stayed with us for a while. When I was a boy. But something happened.'

'What?'

'I forget.'

'She left?'

'I forget. She just disappeared, I think. But I don't know for sure. It happened when I was about seven. I remember that my aunt was very sad. The woman had been her model, you see. There's still some statues of her in my aunt's studio, I think.'

'Can't you remember anything about her?'

'She was beautiful.'

'Yes?'

'And she had the strangest eyes. They looked right through you. Piercing blue eyes. Like stained glass. Oh, I remember her name as well.'

'Was it Petra?' I asked.

'Why, yes. That's right. Do you know her?'

'I'm beginning to,' I answered.

The next morning, at breakfast, I said, 'It's so strange for me to look out of the window and see trees. All I usually see are brick walls.'

'I love it here so much,' said Cromwell. 'I'm really a country boy. My aunt said she felt the same way when she came here for the first time. It used to be a farm then. She was evacuated during the war and came back afterwards.'

'I know.'

'You seem to know a lot about us.'

'Not enough, though. I want to know everything.'

Orpheus pecked at some breadcrumbs on the table. Cromwell clucked his tongue against the roof of his mouth and the bird flew to his shoulder.

'My aunt says that when I was a child I used to talk to the animals. I don't remember that. At least, not all of it. I do remember being surrounded by animals. They used to come to me. I would sit in the forest and they would just come to me. Farmers used me to keep the crows off their fields. I would go to the fields and say something and the birds would fly away. They obeyed me in everything. I was a scarecrow even then. That's what they called me at school, you know. Scarecrow. I think I even started to look like a scarecrow.'

'But you're not,' I said. 'You're not at all.'

'That's what my aunt would say to me.'

I held his hand across the table.

'What did I do before I met you?' I said. 'I can't imagine living without you now. All the old clichés are true, after all.'

'What shall we do today?' he asked.

'Talk,' I said.

We sat in the forest. The earth was damp. The smells were new for me, without memory.

'I often wondered why no one ever liked me at school,' said Cromwell. 'You see, I liked them. At least I didn't hate them. But they hated me. I was always being beaten up in the playground and things like that. One day they dropped a frog down my back and squashed it flat. Oh, I can still feel it. They just wanted to hurt me, there's no explanation for it. They just wanted to make me suffer. It made them feel better. Stronger somehow. Yes. They were stronger for hurting me.'

'Were you sad?'

'Oh, no. I had Aunt Helen. No, I wasn't sad. I was happy. More happy than any of them. No. They didn't bother me. Just puzzled me. I felt sorry for them. You see, I could see them. See them for what they really were.'

'Perhaps that's why they hated you so much.'

'I don't know.'

'What did Helen say?'

'Oh, she said I shouldn't let them bother me.' He smiled. 'She said it was good that I could see beyond all their pettiness.'

I nodded and held him.

'I think I've got something to learn from that,' I said. 'Just to see is not enough. Sometimes you have to see through things. Through and beyond. It's just that I feel trapped.'

'By what?'

'Things in the past.'

'But you weren't part of them.'

'I've become part of them. I'm *making* myself part of them.'

'Why?'

'Because the story never seems to be over,' I answered. 'It just goes on and on. It's endless. And everything is connected.'

'So?'

'I don't know,' I said. 'I just want the thing resolved. Is that too much to ask for?'

'Tell me about yourself,' said Cromwell. 'Speak to me. Tell me things. I want to know everything you've ever done. I want to get inside your skull. I want to know your dreams.'

We lay in bed together. It was our last night alone before Helen was to join us. The window was open and a gentle summer's breeze blew over us.

'My dreams,' I said.

Chapter Sixteen _____

THIS DREAM I remember.

It was night and I was watching television with my parents. Dad was rocking me backwards and forwards in his lap. Suddenly we became aware of noises outside. Screams, cries, running feet.

'What's happening?' I asked.

'Don't know,' said dad. And put me on the floor.

We all went to the front door.

People were running down the street in panic. Some of them were only half-dressed. Everyone looked scared to death.

'Run!' they screamed at us. 'Run!'

'Why?' asked dad.

'The monster, the devil, the infidel is coming,' they screamed at us. 'Can't you feel it? The ground is shaking. We always said it would happen. Now it has.'

'Where is the monster?'

'In that house.' And they pointed down the street. 'In there. He's been hiding in there all these years and we never knew. You've got to run. Run for your lives.'

But we didn't run.

Instead my dad said, 'I'm not afraid. Come on.'

And, hand in hand, we pushed our way through the running mob until we stood in the middle of the street, facing the house.

The road shook beneath our feet. As we looked at the house it started to crack and tremble and bricks fell to the pavement. The windows exploded. Slates fell from the roof and crashed around us.

'No!' cried my mum. 'I can't stay!'

'Stay!' ordered dad. And held her tight. He squashed her hand in his. So tight she yelped with pain. 'You'll stay.'

Suddenly the roof of the house flew off with a thunderous crack. The noise was so devastating I felt sick. And a huge, winged monster rose from inside the house. Hundreds of feet high. A gigantic gargoyle with yellow fangs and talons, dripping with locusts and rats, flies and maggots crawling in every pore of its hideous body.

Gradually, the monster turned and looked down. It saw us. An evil smile stretched its lips.

And then it started to point. A huge, deformed, infested finger of accusation started to move towards us.

It's going to point at my mother, I thought. Yes. This is it. At last. Now everyone will know her for what she is.

But it didn't.

The monster pointed at me.

Chapter Seventeen ⎯⎯⎯

HELEN SAT DOWN opposite me at the kitchen table.
Cromwell had gone to bed.

She took the tea-bags from the cups and poured in some milk. She handed me a cup and smiled.

'You've been having a good time here, eh?' she asked.

'Oh, yes,' I said.

'Cromwell looks wonderful. You've been good for him, Connie. I'm grateful to you for that. I thought I might be losing him somehow. But you've brought him back.'

I sipped my tea.

'You know . . .' I began.

'What?'

'Mama Zep told me things.'

'Things?'

'About what happened.'

The expression on her face didn't change. She just stared at me. Waiting.

'Yes?' she said.

'Things that happened before. My mum, Cromwell's mum.'

'Yes. I thought so.'

'So why didn't you tell me. You knew as well. Why didn't you tell me about Petra Gerda?'

'What about her?'

˙About her living here with you.'

Helen sighed and lay back in the chair. The wood creaked beneath her weight. She stared into the steam of her tea.

'Oh, I don't know. Why did Zep tell you all this? Why? What possible good can it do? She's just a meddling old harpy. Listen, Connie. You can keep on pushing and pushing this if you want to. It goes on for as long as you want it to go on. Stories don't stop. They just become other stories.'

'Exactly,' I said. 'That's just the point. And now it's become my story. That's why I can't let it go. It started as the story of Mama Zep and her ability to see ghosts, then it was Mama Zep and Judge, then Jessica and Gabriel, then Rachel and Petra, then Judge and Steven, then my mum. And now I've joined in. I've become part of it all. Don't you see that? It's the story of Cromwell and I now. Of me and Cromwell. You're right. It does go on and on. It's for that reason I can't let go. I'm going to hold on until it makes some sense.'

'You're going to have a long wait if you want it to make sense, my boy.' She drank some tea.

There was a pause. 'Tell me,' I said, 'about Petra.'

'Oh, Petra,' said Helen softly. 'Well she didn't come here to see me. You must understand that. She came to see Cromwell. The baby Cromwell. He was her one remaining link with Rachel, you see. And she still loved Rachel.'

'What was she like?'

'Petra?'

'Yes.'

'Oh, how can I say. Petra was all things to all people. People saw in her what they wanted to see. She was a kind of mirror for them. A way of seeing things.'

'What was she for you?'

'Someone I loved. Someone that loved me. I fell in love with her the first time I saw her. Like you fell for Cromwell. And I've loved her ever since. There's no escaping love like that.'

'A lot of people seemed to love and hate her.'

'Yes. She was that kind of person.' She looked at me and smiled. 'Do you want to know what happened, Concord Webster? Do you want to know what happened to Petra Gerda?'

'Oh, tell me,' I said.

'She came here to see Cromwell. She was devastated. Over Rachel. But she soon got over it. Once she was here that is. That was all part of Petra. Oh, I was so in love with her. My life made sense when I was her lover. She stayed here for seven years. What can I say about those years? I lived them and that's it. Cromwell grew up. Petra spoke about your mother and Judge and Rachel. How she had been deceived. How she should have done this and that. But didn't. And so life trickles away. Vaguely.

'She went missing on Cromwell's seventh birthday. She had been in an odd mood all day. Distant somehow.' She looked out of the window. 'We went for a walk in the forest. I remember Cromwell was playing. Hiding in the piles of leaves. It was his favourite game. He would bury himself and we had to find him. Then it was Petra's turn. I watched her. Watched her fall into a pile of leaves. They covered her. She was completely buried. She waved at me and smiled before the leaves covered her. A strange smile. Then we had to go and find her.'

'Only you didn't.'

'No,' said Helen. And looked at me. 'No. We didn't find her. We scattered the leaves around us. I grew frantic and screamed her name. But she was gone. I haven't seen her since. I think she'd simply had enough, you see. She crawled into the leaves and willed herself to disappear.'

'I'm sorry,' I said.

'Yes. So am I.' She stared at me. 'Strange. Before you came I

could sense the same thing happening to Cromwell. He was
becoming invisible. Right before my eyes.'

'But now he's back.'

'Yes.' Reaching for my hand. 'Oh, yes.'

'But there's still something else,' I said.

'How do you mean?'

'The little starling.'

She looked me in the eyes.

'Steven Feather,' she whispered.

'Yes. Steven Feather.'

'Oh, you must leave it alone, Con. It won't do you any good.'

'I have to know.'

'You don't.'

'Yes,' I said. 'I do.'

'But this is nothing to do with you. Really. Nothing.'

'My mum told Steven's parents.'

She nodded.

'She ruined it for the two boys.'

'Yes.'

'And Steven ran away.'

'But . . .'

'He came here, didn't he?'

She nodded.

'Is he alive now?'

'Yes,' she said. 'He's alive.'

'And you know where he is?'

'Yes.'

'I want to see him, Helen. I have to talk to him. I have to find out
things. Will you tell me where he is?'

She let go of my hand and stood up.

'And what do you think that's going to achieve, Connie? You're
letting it drag you down. Why do it? It's over.'

'But it's not over. It's still going on. It's going on in me and Cromwell. If we are the last link then I want to make it mean something. I want to change things.'

'Oh,' she murmured. 'Change.'

'I want Cromwell to meet Steven.'

'Oh, what possible good can that do?'

'He's Judge Martin's son.'

'I'm well aware of that.' She sat down as if exhausted. 'Oh, Connie, Connie, Connie.'

'Steven Feather. Where is he?'

'You're thinking only of yourself,' she said.

'I know that.'

A pause.

'What do you think Steven can tell you that you don't already know?'

'Secrets,' I replied.

'That would be a terrible thing to do.'

Another pause.

'Will you tell me?' I asked.

'Mmm.'

Chapter Eighteen _____

CROMWELL AND I walked along the beach and licked our ice-creams. The sky was an endless, flat blue. The sand was covered with holiday-makers.

'What *are* you looking for?' asked Cromwell.

'What do you mean?'

'Your eyes are darting all over the place. Have you lost something?'

'Oh.' I laughed. 'No. It's not that. It's the first time I've been here. I just want to take everything in.'

'Well, you're certainly doing that.'

The seagulls shrieked above our heads, flecks of white against the blue. Sand and pebbles got into our shoes as we worked our way through the maze of deck-chairs.

'Oh, let's go back,' said Cromwell.

'Why?'

'I'm getting sunburnt.'

'Not yet,' I said.

'What is wrong with you?'

'Don't you like it here?'

'No. I don't.'

'Listen,' I said, trying to calm him down. 'There's a Punch and Judy show somewhere. We'll see that and then we'll go. Okay?'

'But I don't want . . .'

'Please, Crom. Then we'll go. I promise.'

He sighed and walked along beside me.

After our ice-creams had melted down our fingers and arms we bought some candyfloss. Sucking at the pink fuzz put Cromwell in a better mood. He started to laugh and held my hand.

Orpheus pecked lightly at the floss.

We laughed.

Then I saw it.

'There!' I exclaimed. 'There it is!'

Set back from the beach, in a little concrete arena, a Punch and Judy show was already in progress. Children sat watching.

I pushed Cromwell forward so that he could have a good view. I stood slightly behind him, to his left, and waited. A few parents complained that we were spoiling their children's view. But I didn't listen to them.

Punch was hitting Judy.

See him, I thought. See him.

Punch and the crocodile.

Oh, see him.

The crocodile alone, sausages in mouth.

And then the crocodile stared out into the audience and seemed to see Cromwell. Its mouth hung open and the sausages fell to the floor. A few children giggled and looked at Cromwell, expecting him to do something, as if he was part of the show.

The crocodile stared at Cromwell.

Yes, I thought. It is him. I have brought him to you. Those we lose but still love with all our heart we shall meet again.

'What's going on?' murmured Cromwell.

But, by now, the show was back to normal. The children sat enthralled as if nothing had happened.

The show finished and the children dispersed.

'Come on,' said Cromwell. 'Let's go.'

'Wait a second,' I said.

I stared at the striped Punch and Judy box. There was movement inside the canvas womb.

Come out, I said. Come out.

Then a flap opened at the side and a little man appeared. He was completely bald with a glowing red face. He was dressed in a striped blue and white T-shirt and white trousers.

Wiping his hands on a towel he came over to us.

'Well, well, well,' he murmured.

'Hello,' I said.

'You look so much like your father,' he said to Cromwell. 'When he was your age.'

'Helen told me where to find you,' I said.

He nodded.

'You see,' I began, 'Judge is dead. I found his body. Mama Zep and I found his body.'

'Dead?' Steven frowned. 'Dead?'

'I've been hearing all these stories,' I continued. 'And I had to come and see you. You see, I'm in love with Cromwell.'

'So I see,' he said.

'And I have to know things.'

'What things?'

'I don't know. That's just it. All I do is listen. Listen to stories. But they don't make any sense. They just go on and on. They keep changing.'

'And now you've become part of that story.'

'Yes. Exactly.' I paused.

'Well?'

'My mother . . .'

'Yes?'

'She told your parents. About you and Judge.'

'Yes. So?'

'Oh, I have to know!'

'Mmm. Well.' He gave an embarrassed chuckle. 'You nearly held up the show there, eh?'

'You know each other?' asked Cromwell.

'Oh, yes,' I said. 'Very well.' I held out my hand. 'I'm Concord Webster,' I said.

'Well, well, well.' He looked at Cromwell. 'You're Judge Martin's boy, aren't you.'

'Yes,' said Cromwell.

'I've come a long way to see you,' I said.

'Well. Yes. No doubt,' he said. 'Come back home, then. I suppose you want to talk?'

'Yes,' I said.

'What's going on?' asked Cromwell.

'This is Steven Feather,' I explained.

And waited.

Cromwell blinked.

'I loved your father,' said Steven. 'Years ago.'

Steven's house was full of dolls and puppets. We sat in the living-room and drank lemonade. He couldn't take his eyes off Cromwell.

'What is there to know? Your mother told my parents. There it is. Only she wasn't your mother then. She told them and all hell was let loose.'

'My mother broke it all to pieces for you.'

'Well, she . . .'

'My mother . . .'

'Oh, your mother this and your mother that. What makes you think your precious little mother was so important in all this? What was your mother? She was nothing. Nothing. No one cared anything for your mother. Oh, I felt sorry for her. We all did in a way. That's why we trusted her so much, I suppose. We just never took her seriously. She was just there. She was used. Used by everyone. Everyone. And she needed us all so much. Oh, poor Faith Niven. None of us blamed her. Not really. You see, she had nothing. Nothing. And when she thought she was losing the little she did have – Rachel – she just went mad.

'In the end, as it turned out, I proved myself weaker than her. I ran away. But . . . well, my parents made it a nightmare for me. I couldn't stay. They locked me in a cupboard. Do you know that? They locked me in a cupboard like a wild animal. It was terrible. I had to run away. But I saw Judge before I left. We met in secret. I begged him to run away with me.'

'You met him before you left?'

'Oh, yes. No one ever knew. We had a secret place, you see. No one knew of its existence. Not as far as we knew. It was an old empty house. We called this place the Castle. Judge and I spent a night there together. I begged him to leave. To come with me. But he wouldn't.'

'Because of Rachel.'

'Oh, no. Rachel had nothing to do with it. It was because of his mother. He wouldn't leave his mother, Jessica. She was ill, you see. She needed looking after. And Judge wouldn't leave. Oh, he was fond of Rachel, yes. But she had nothing to do with it. And so, he stayed, and I left. And that was that. You see how easy it is to live a life. Hardly anything at all. You close one eye and blink with the other and all your life is over.'

'But other people's lives still go on,' I said. 'Other people are left to pick up the pieces. And make sense of it all.'

'Make sense of it! Oh dear, oh dear. Is that why you're here? To make sense of it all? Listen to me. You want to know why things happened? I'll tell you. Because people didn't know themselves. That's why.'

I looked into Steven's eyes. There were sparks there.

'Tell me about him,' I said. 'Judge Martin. What was he like?'

Steven smiled.

'Oh, he was a joy,' he said. 'Quite simply. A joy. What else can I say? He was so beautiful. Sometimes I can still feel his body. But people tore us apart.'

'My mother.'

'No. Not your mother. Why are you so intent on this? Why must you point the finger?'

I held his hand. It was smooth. Like a boy's hand. The nails were long and clean.

'And Petra?' I asked.

'What about her?'

'What was she like?'

'Oh, wonderful. She could have taught us, I think. But even she was deceived in the end.'

'By my moth—'

'No! Don't keep dragging your mother into this. Petra was deceived by herself. She was both too wise and too innocent. We all have to know a Petra Gerda once in our lives.'

'Helen said she fell into a pile of leaves and was never found again.'

'Yes, well, that sounds about right to me. Perhaps she found a secret doorway into another world and slipped into it. A rabbit hole into another kingdom.'

'Was she ever happy?'

'Petra? Who knows. I think she was when I knew her. But, I think, she was too wise to be happy. She could see all the ignorance around her. You can't see all that and still be happy. But tell me. You see, I want to know something now. Tell me about Faith.'

'My mother? Why?'

'Well, I know what happened to the rest of us. I took a photograph once . . .'

'I've seen it. Judge is looking at you through a window. And the three girls are there. Rachel, Faith and my mother. Your shadow is in the photograph. It falls across my mother.'

'Oh, you say that with such relish. What a melodramatic little Concord Webster you are. It falls across your mother, does it? Is that the way you see it all, then? Your mother living under my shadow all these years? Is that what's been at the back of your mind?'

'Something like that.'

'Oh, silly, silly boy. Tell me about Faith.'

'Well, she married. Ronnie Webster.'

'I don't know him.'

'He came after you.'

'Have you any brothers or sisters?'

'No.'

'Is Faith happy?'

'I don't know.'

'Did she appear happy?'

'Yes. Until . . .'

'Until?'

'Until Judge died.'

'Did she ever speak to Judge? Afterwards?'

'No. She always said she hated him. She taught us to hate him. She called him names. The Devil.'

'I see. Yes.' He gripped my hand tight. 'Oh, don't you see? Don't you see how much she's hated herself all these years?'

'I suppose.'

'But she loves you.'

'Yes,' I said.

'And you love her?'

'Yes. But . . .'

'But what?'

'But how can I? Knowing what she is? Knowing what she's done?'

'If you love her enough you can teach her. Teach her what she might be. Help her forget.'

I stood up and walked round the room, touching the various puppets and dolls. On a chair in the corner there sat a little gargoyle. It was hideous.

'What's this one?' I asked.

'Ah.' Steven stood up. 'That's my favourite.' He grabbed the puppet. 'It's the oldest thing here. It was the first puppet I made after I ran away.' He stuck his hand into a hole in the back. The monster's face turned to look at me. 'This,' announced Steven, 'is Mr Fury. Say hello to Mr Fury.'

'Hello, Mr Fury,' I said.

'Hello,' cackled the demon, its mouth opening to reveal yellow fangs. 'What's your name?'

'Concord Webster.'

'What a good name,' it went on. 'Look into my eyes, Concord Webster. Look into my eyes and tell me what you see.'

I stared.

His eyes were two pieces of broken mirror.

'What do you see?' it asked.

'Myself,' I answered.

Steven put the gargoyle down and looked at me.

'Exactly,' he said. And smiled.

Chapter Nineteen _____

'I WANT TO show you something,' said Helen.

She took me up to her studio. It smelt of clay and dust. She took me to a dark corner and pulled a sheet from a statue.

It was a woman.

'This was the last thing I ever did of her,' she said. 'This is Petra Gerda.'

I stared into the grey stone face. The eyes were two holes. I trembled all over.

'And this . . .' said Helen. And showed me a plaster head. 'It's a life mask, if you like. I made a cast of Petra's head while she was still with me.'

I touched it.

'That's all there is left,' said Helen. 'It's her but not her. You know why I'm showing you these things, don't you?'

'Yes,' I said.

'Good. Then there's still a chance.'

Part Five

Opening the Devil's Door

Chapter Twenty _____

LOVERBOY TALLIS SAW the devil on his eighteenth birthday. He saw it in the face of his best friend. The shock made him disappear.

It was early morning when we got back home. The street felt different somehow. As if someone had painted everything in slightly faded colours while I had been away. I mentioned this to Cromwell, but he didn't seem to think so. Probably because he hadn't lived on the street as I had done. The place hadn't become part of him. Places can become as real as people sometimes, eat their way into your skull, develop an identity. I hadn't realized just how much I had become part of the place where I had been born. Until I met Cromwell Martin and discovered areas of my own mind that had not been infested.

We went straight to Cromwell's house and made some tea. There was a slight chill in the air so we lit the oven to keep warm. Cromwell looked tired.

'Are you okay?' I asked.

'You know,' he said, 'I really don't want to know anything. About the past and things. About what happened before. I know it concerns my dad and your mum. But I don't feel it's part of me. I don't want it to be part of me. Not at all. It confuses me. Scares me in a way.'

'Okay,' I said. 'I shouldn't have taken you to see Steven Feather. I'm sorry.'

'Oh, no. I'm glad you did that. But what he had to say didn't mean anything to me. That's all. He was a nice old guy. I liked him. Perhaps we'll visit him again.'

'Perhaps. If you want to.'

'Oh, I don't know what I want. That's just it.'

'I see,' I said.

The house was completely bare. Helen had got rid of everything that had belonged to Judge Martin. She had stripped the walls and whitewashed them. Being inside the house was like living inside a huge, bleached skeleton.

I stood up and looked at my reflection in the mirror.

'God!' I said. 'I look terrible.'

'You're tired,' said Cromwell.

'I don't feel it. I'm too restless. As if something's going to happen and I don't know what.' I touched my hair.

I sat beside him and put my arm round his shoulders. I kissed the nape of his neck. The tick of his pulse throbbed against my lips. My fingers touched him gently, as if the slightest pressure would bruise him beyond repair.

'I'm going to sleep all day and all night,' said Cromwell.

'Do that,' I whispered into his ear. 'Then I'll come and wake you.'

When I got home mum and dad were having breakfast. They glanced up as I walked into the kitchen. Mum had been to the hairdresser's while I'd been away. She was back to her usual self. A cigarette dangled from the corner of her mouth.

'The prodigal son,' murmured dad. And continued reading the newspaper.

Mum stood up and stared at me. There was something hard and glinting in her eyes. She took the cigarette from her mouth and breathed smoke at me.

'Do you want something?' she asked.

'I'm hungry,' I said.

'Sit down.'

I sat beside dad.

'Did you have a good time?' he asked.

'It was okay.'

'Nice place?'

'Yes.'

'See any pheasants?'

'No.'

'Did you look?'

'Not really.'

'What did you do, then?'

'Just lazed around.'

'With the Martin kid?'

'With Cromwell, yes.'

'I see,' said dad. Then looked at the clock. 'I'll be late. I promised to pick Dicky up on my way to work. He'll murder me if I'm late.'

'Oh,' I said. 'Are you and Dicky talking again?'

Dad looked at me and frowned.

'What's that supposed to mean?'

'I thought you weren't talking to Dicky Tallis.'

'Don't talk crap.'

'But you said . . .'

'Look here, son. I've had just about enough of your little sarcasms in this house. I'm not one of your kids in the street, you know. And I'm not your mother neither. You can't talk to me how you damn well want to. You treat me with some respect or you're *out*. Do you hear me? Out!'

'Oh, don't start, Ron,' said mum.

'And you can keep out of it as well. Just because you let him talk to you like dirt. He strolls in here as casual as you like. Uses the fucking place like a hotel, treats us like the bloody servants. Well,

I'm not going to stand for it. Do you hear me? I'm not going to stand for it.'

'But before I left,' I said. 'You told me that I wasn't to speak to Loverboy . . .'

'Shut it, son! I'm warning you! Shut it or I'll do something I'll be sorry for. I warn you!'

There was a pause. For a second I thought he was going to hit me. A real punch. As if I wasn't his son at all. Just someone he wanted to hurt.

'You'll be late,' said mum. And gave him his lunch in a brown paper bag. 'You'd best get going.'

As he got to the front door he turned.

'You want to know something!' he called back at me. 'You take everything too seriously. That's your trouble. Both of you. You're like peas in a pod. There's no humour in either of you.'

He slammed the door shut.

'Ignore him,' said mum, putting some scrambled eggs on toast in front of me. 'He's just embarrassed, that's all.'

'Embarrassed?'

'Because he's friends with Dicky again.' She sat down and lit another cigarette. 'When he comes home and casually tells me he's been out drinking with Dicky again, I just smile and nod and ask him if he's had a good time. That's the way to handle him. I know better than to question him. Just let him get on with it. Men. They're always little boys. They never grow up.'

We sat in silence for a while.

I ate my breakfast.

Mum watched me the whole time.

After I had finished I smiled at her.

She smiled back and blew smoke rings.

I laughed.

'You're still good at that,' I said.

'Old tricks die hard.'

'Your hair looks nice.'

'One has to make an effort.'

'Did it cost much?'

'No. Angela did it for me.'

'It looks great.'

'Well, it hides the grey.'

'Are you going grey?'

'Oh, for years.'

'I'm sorry.'

'Oh, there's nothing you can do about it.'

'No. Not your hair. For what I said.'

'I see,' she said.

'I'm sorry for everything.'

'Yes,' she murmured. 'So am I.'

'It's just that . . .'

'What?'

'I don't know. It's just that I'm finding it hard to see you somehow. I don't know how.'

She threw the cigarette into her half-empty coffee-cup. It sizzled.

'I've been thinking,' she said. 'While you've been gone. I've done a lot of thinking. And I've decided to explain nothing to you. And do you know why? Because I can't explain it to myself. That's why. I wish I could, Con. But I can't.'

'I met Steven Feather,' I said.

She stared at me.

'How?'

'Helen Martin told me where to find him.'

'Steven Feather,' she said. 'Well. How is . . .?'

'Oh, fine. Really. He asked me how you were.'

'It's been years.'

'I liked him a lot.'

'Yes,' said my mum. 'I liked him a lot too.'

There is an old photograph, brown and faded, curling at
the edges. In this photograph there are three young women, still girls
in a way. Petra Gerda, Rachel Sims, and Faith Niven. Petra and
Rachel are staring at the camera. Faith Niven is looking at them. To
the left of the photograph there is a window. Behind the window
can be seen a face. It is a young man, still a boy in a way. He has jet-
black hair scraped back from his forehead, pale skin, dark eyes. This
is Judge Martin. He is looking at the camera, at the person taking the
photograph. He is looking and there is love in his eyes. Hope. A
sense of the future. From the bottom of the photograph there rises a
shadow. This shadow falls across Faith Niven. It is the shadow cast
by Steven Feather. She is unaware of the shadow because she is
looking at her friends. In this photograph a moment in time was
captured when all things could have been wonderful. Judge was
going to run away with Steven, Petra was in love with Rachel.
Everything could have been magical. But it didn't work out like
that. And when the shutter clicked on that single moment it must
have reverberated with the sound of doom.

I went to see Loverboy Tallis.
We sat in his bedroom talking.
'The Castle was lonely without you,' he said.
'Yes,' I said.
There was a slight pause. There was an awkward feeling between
us. The sound of breaking glass.
'I'm in love,' I said.
'With Cromwell.'
'Yes.'
'I thought so. When I saw him in the Castle I knew. So where
does that leave me?'

'I don't understand, Tal.'

'Then let me explain. Here I am still trying to convince Angel to marry me . . .'

'But why convince her?'

'What else can I do?'

'Do you want . . .?'

'My parents will go mad if I don't marry her after all this time.'

'But Tal . . .'

'Are you going to leave me for Cromwell Martin?'

'I'm not leaving you.'

'Do your parents know?'

'Know?'

'About you?'

'How do you mean?'

'About you and Cromwell Martin.'

'I don't know,' I said.

'I see.'

'Why?'

'Nothing.'

'Why, Tal?'

'Nothing. It's my birthday tomorrow.'

'I know.'

'We're having a party after all. Our dads are friends again. All is well, eh?'

'Yes,' I said.

'I'm going to see Angel tonight. She's baby-sitting again. Yes? I'm going to make her decide what she wants to do. Yes? You see I want to make the announcement at the birthday party.'

'The announcement?'

'About the engagement,' he said.

'What's wrong with you, Tal. You're different.'

'Am I? Does it scare you?'

'Yes,' I said. 'It does.'
'Oh, poor Concord. Poor, poor Concord.'

I went to Cromwell's house.

I put the key in the lock and opened the door. The hallway was white and smelt of pine. I went upstairs and touched the bedroom door.

It swung open, silently, as if by magic.

How can I describe my love? Words are impossible, you see. Is it enough to say that I loved him? No. That is not enough. And so, in the end, the event is rendered useless and meaningless.

The room was lit by a gentle, evening twilight. A shaft of amber twilight fell through a gap in the curtains illuminating the bed.

He lay there like an angel. He was naked and his white body was shimmering with golden life. As I watched, a ladybird crawled across his cheek.

I walked over to the bed and kissed him.

He opened his eyes.

Chapter Twenty-one _____

IN THE MORNING I left Cromwell in bed.

As I walked down the street Mama Zep tapped on her window and called me inside.

'Have you heard?' she asked.

'Heard what?'

'Didn't you hear the sirens last night?'

'No,' I said.

'All love is deaf, I suppose.'

'What happened?'

'There was trouble,' she said. 'At Angela Calvert's house.'

'Angela? What happened?'

'I haven't found it all out yet. But . . .'

'What?'

'She tried to kill Paul, I think. From what I can tell. She tried to kill her own brother. They think he's blind. She threw bleach in his eyes. He's in hospital now.'

'And Angela?'

'At home.'

I rushed out of the house.

I knocked on the front door.

Sheila Calvert opened it.

'Connie,' she said. She looked like death warmed up. Eyes blood-shot and swollen.

'I've just heard,' I said.

'Oh. Yes.'

'How is he?'

'They're not sure.'

'Can they save his eyes?'

'They don't know yet.' And she started to cry.

I helped her into the kitchen. We sat down. She sobbed into an old tea-towel.

'Frank's at the hospital now,' she said. 'I'm just going there myself. Oh, Con. You should see him. His little face. I'll never forget it as long as I live. Oh, God.'

'Where is Angela now?'

'Upstairs. In her room.'

'Can I see her?'

'You can do what you like with her. She's no daughter of mine. I don't want her in this house any more. I want her out.'

'Sheila . . .'

'She's a witch, Connie. A witch.'

'No, Sheila.'

'A witch!'

I knocked on Angel's door.

There was no answer.

I went inside.

She was sitting in a chair beside the bed, staring at the wall. Her face was blank and expressionless. She didn't even glance at me as I sat in front of her.

'Angela?'

No answer.

'Angela?'

She looked at me.

'I don't know how I did it,' she said. 'I just did.'

'Tell me.'

'I've told everyone a million times.'

'But not me,' I said.

'Oh, Loverboy was here. We were up in this room. Paul was asleep. Wheezing. Oh, his bloody wheezing. And Loverboy and I were sitting on the bed. Talking. Oh, the talking. On and on. He just didn't stop talking. On and on. About how we should do this and do that. About what people would do if we didn't. What would the street say, he asked me. What would the street say? Oh, God. And we got into a fight. A real fight. A real screaming match. Loverboy rushed out. And Paul wakes up. And wheezes at me, wheezes. Oh, God help me. The next thing I knew I had thrown . . . thrown the . . .'

'Angela.' I held her hand.

'No,' she said, pulling her hand away. 'Hadn't you heard? I'm not Angel any more. I'm a witch.'

'No,' I said.

'My mum told me. A witch.'

'Don't believe that,' I said.

'What else is there?' she asked.

As soon as I got home I knew something was wrong. Mum and dad were in the living-room.

'Have you heard about . . .' I began.

'I know,' said dad. 'That's nothing. Loverboy came here.'

'Oh?'

'He told us some things.'

'About Angela?'

'No. About you.'

'Oh?'

'About you and Cromwell Martin.'

'Oh?'

'Is it true?' asked my dad.

'Yes,' I said.

Dad rushed over to me and grabbed me around the neck. The force of it hurled me against the wall. I cracked my head against the light switch with a sickening thud.

'I want you out of this house,' he snarled at me. 'Do you hear me? Out of this house.'

I thought he was going to strangle me.

Mum pushed him off.

'Take your hands off him!' she screamed.

He raised his fist at her.

'Don't you fucking well dare lay a hand on me, Ronald Webster,' she said. 'Don't you dare! Me or him. Touch him one more time and I'll have your eyes out, I swear I will.'

'You take his side!'

'Oh, get out!' she screamed at him. 'I'll stab you in your sleep. I swear I will.'

'Oh, fuck the both of you!' shouted dad.

And stormed out.

'Are you okay?' asked mum.

I nodded.

She cried and held me.

'Where is Loverboy now?' I asked.

'No one knows. Ivy was here earlier. He hasn't been seen since last night. He must have come here after he left Angela's. Since then he hasn't been heard of.'

'I'm going to find him,' I said.

Mum held my hand.

'It's alright,' I assured her. 'Nothing's broken.'

★

When I got to the Castle Loverboy was wearing the dragon mask.

'What are you playing at?' I asked.

'What do you mean?'

'All this going to my parents. Have you any idea what happened last night? After you left Angela?'

'Yes. It's not my fault.'

'I didn't say it was your fault. But it's still part of you, Tal. Part of all of us.'

He turned away from me.

I rushed over and grabbed him.

'I thought you were my friend!' I shouted.

The dragon's eyes looked at me.

'I trusted you, Tal.'

'Why?'

'I . . . I . . .' Because I couldn't speak I pushed him to the floor. 'You bastard!' I screamed.

I punched him.

I knelt across his chest and punched him again and again. The dragon mask disintegrated under my relentless anger. Loverboy's face was covered in blood. And still I punched.

He tried to fight back but his arms were trapped under my knees.

Finally, exhausted, I crawled off him and staggered to the sofa. I fell on it and started to cry.

There was a silence.

Loverboy got to his feet. He stared at me. He spat blood on to the floor.

'Underneath,' he said. 'All the time. You're like all the rest. There's no difference.'

'Tal . . .' I began.

'I'm not wanted here.'

I looked at him.

He seemed to smile at me.

I blinked, just once, and when I opened my eyes Loverboy had gone. It was as if he had never been. The crushed dragon mask lay where he had stood.

I sat in silence for a while.

'I thought you'd be here,' said a voice.

Cromwell sat beside me.

I lay helpless against him. He tried to comfort me.

Suddenly, I heard a strange, scraping noise. Something was moving across the floor. At first I thought it might be rats. I sat up in alarm. But no. Not rats.

I looked at Cromwell.

Red stars sparkled around his head like a halo of comets. And from all over the room there came a million different scraping noises, glass against wood.

From every corner of the room bits of blue glass were emerging, drawn towards Cromwell as if he were a magnet. He held out his hand. And, like film in reverse, the blue dolphin became whole again, the shattered image coming together in Cromwell's outstretched hand.

He gave it to me.

'Yes,' I said. And smiled.

That night Cromwell wet my hair. It hung round my shoulders in rat-tails. Then he picked up the scissors and, for a while, stood in front of me staring at them.

'What's wrong?' I asked.

'It's such a shame,' he replied, softly.

'Why?'

'Your hair's so beautiful. It must have taken years to grow it this long.'

'Just do it,' I said. 'Please.'

Carefully he started to cut my hair. Then, when it was short enough – nothing more than an uneven stubble – he rubbed shaving foam over my scalp.

He picked up the razor.

Again he hesitated.

'Hurry up,' I said. 'My head's itching.'

Cromwell scraped the razor through the stubble. Lumps of hair and shaving foam fell to the floor like tiny red turds. When my skull was shaven and smooth I looked at myself in the mirror. The newly revealed skin was whiter than the rest of me. My skull felt new and tender, vulnerable.

I looked so different. It scared me. This wasn't me at all. The thought of it thrilled me.

Cromwell came up behind me.

'Happy?' he asked.

'I don't know,' I replied.

Opening the living-room door I faced mum and dad.

'Sweet Jesus!' hissed dad, and stood up.

'I'm just showing you,' I said.

'You look . . .'

'I don't care what you think,' I said. 'You're beyond me. I'm just showing you. You can think what you like. Call me what you like. I just thought you should know.'

Mum stood up.

'Thank you,' she said, softly.

I smiled.

'I just thought you should see,' I said. And turned my back on them.

'It's that boy's influence,' my dad said. 'I know it. I forbid you to see him. It's all his fault, the little bastard. I forbid you to go in that house again.'

I left them.

Outside the stars were bright in the night sky. I felt safe and wonderful as I walked down the street. Yes, I thought. Yes. There is still a chance. No one can stop me from entering the house. No one will stop me from opening the door.

I have the key.

FOR THE BEST IN PAPERBACKS, LOOK FOR THE

In every corner of the world, on every subject under the sun, Penguin represents quality and variety – the very best in publishing today.

For complete information about books available from Penguin – including Pelicans, Puffins, Peregrines and Penguin Classics – and how to order them, write to us at the appropriate address below. Please note that for copyright reasons the selection of books varies from country to country.

In the United Kingdom: Please write to *Dept E.P., Penguin Books Ltd, Harmondsworth, Middlesex, UB7 0DA*

In the United States: Please write to *Dept BA, Penguin, 299 Murray Hill Parkway, East Rutherford, New Jersey 07073*

In Canada: Please write to *Penguin Books Canada Ltd, 2801 John Street, Markham, Ontario L3R 1B4*

In Australia: Please write to the *Marketing Department, Penguin Books Australia Ltd, P.O. Box 257, Ringwood, Victoria 3134*

In New Zealand: Please write to the *Marketing Department, Penguin Books (NZ) Ltd, Private Bag, Takapuna, Auckland 9*

In India: Please write to *Penguin Overseas Ltd, 706 Eros Apartments, 56 Nehru Place, New Delhi, 110019*

In Holland: Please write to *Penguin Books Nederland B.V., Postbus 195, NL–1380AD Weesp, Netherlands*

In Germany: Please write to *Penguin Books Ltd, Friedrichstrasse 10–12, D–6000 Frankfurt Main 1, Federal Republic of Germany*

In Spain: Please write to *Longman Penguin España, Calle San Nicolas 15, E–28013 Madrid, Spain*

In France: Please write to *Penguin Books Ltd, 39 Rue de Montmorency, F-75003, Paris, France*

In Japan: Please write to *Longman Penguin Japan Co Ltd, Yamaguchi Building, 2–12–9 Kanda Jimbocho, Chiyoda-Ku, Tokyo 101, Japan*